Three of Hearts

Neal Wooten

ISBN 978-1-61225-094-6

Published in the United States
by Mirror Publishing
Milwaukee, WI 53214

Printed in the USA.

FOR MY MOM

Next exit 18 miles.

The faded green road sign was rusting around the edges and over time the wind had skewed the post so that now, instead of facing the oncoming traffic, the sign seemed to actually point the way to the exit.

I wondered how far down on the list of priorities it was for the Department of Transportation to replace insignificant signs like this one.

It was important to me, though. It told me that I had but one exit to go before I arrived at my destination and it was only 18 miles away.

It was 18 miles to Fort Payne, a small town in the northeast corner of Alabama that had gotten its name from an old Indian fort and later had become one of the thirteen prison camps which housed the Cherokee Indians before they were marched off to Oklahoma on the Trail of Tears. It was a town that now boasted to having more hosiery mills than any other town in America; it was a place where people still sat on their front porch in the evenings and still waved as you passed.

It was also a dry county meaning that they had never embraced the laws of prohibition enacted in the 1920s so buying liquor or even beer was out of the question. If you wanted something to drink, you had to drive to Georgia or

Etowah County, or go to church and ask the bootlegger sitting on the pew beside the city councilman.

Protestant churches adorned the valley in numbers which almost matched the hosiery mills.

It's also a nature lover's paradise surrounded by natural wonders like the Tennessee River, Little River Canyon, and Sequoyah Caverns.

Eighteen miles to home.

Eleven years ago I had moved to Montgomery, the capital of Alabama, which is 200 miles south, and yet I still refer to this area as home. I'm not sure if it is the geographic beauty or the genuine goodness of the people that continues to lure me to this place, but whatever the reason, coming home after several years excited my senses and lit up my memory like nothing else could.

I decided to get off at the first exit and drive through town before heading up to my parent's home. Normally I would take the next exit and it would be a short drive up Sylvania Gap Road to where my parents lived atop Sand Mountain and where the best tomatoes in the world are grown.

Fort Payne rests in the valley where Sand Mountain and Lookout Mountain run parallel to each other and is like traveling back in time as you coast along with the beautiful view of the mountains on each side of town. Being that it was springtime added more beauty as the brown and yellow trees were now polka-dotted with patches of green as the mountains literally seemed to come to life after winter.

I could also tell by getting off at that first exit that the town was thriving with new constructions going up everywhere. There were new restaurants, small shopping centers, a Super Wal-Mart, and of course, new hosiery mills.

The hosiery mills contribute to most of Fort Payne's economy. They had first begun back in the mid 1800s and actually still use the same equipment designed and patented from that period. A few of the larger mills did everything from knitting the yarn into socks, sewing the toes, trimming away the extra threads, dying, boarding, and all the way through to packaging and shipping. Most of the smaller mills, and there were a lot of those, only did the first couple of steps and then sold their products to the larger mills who then completed the process.

A lot of people made a decent living working in the hosiery business. My mom, two sisters, and almost all of my relatives worked in hosiery mills. My brother-in-law had worked for the same mill since he was 15 years old and was now the supervisor of the entire plant. If I had to guess, I would say that one-half of the country's supply of socks came out of Fort Payne. The mills were always hiring so if you couldn't find a job, it's because you weren't looking.

Turning on to Main Street at the South Y, the intersection where Highway 35 meets Gault Avenue at a y-shaped angle, brought a smile to my face as a flood of memories washed over me. My old stomping grounds where most of my late teen years were spent cruising up and down this strip every weekend.

I laugh now wondering if it was a bigger waste of time or gas. My only consolation is the fact that everyone else was doing the same thing.

We would just drive from one end of town to the other, which was only about a five mile drive, then turn around and drive back through. If you saw someone you knew, you said "hello" by flashing your brake lights when they passed while keeping your eyes on the rear view mirror to see them say "hello" back. If you wanted to talk with someone, you followed the brake lights with a turning signal indicating that you wanted them to pull over. A return signal was a mutual agreement meaning they would pull over and wait for you to turn around and come back to them. It was the person that signaled first that always turned around to come back. We did have rules; it wasn't total chaos.

As I neared the North Y, I could see the old canopy of the Shell Car Wash. As it came fully into view, I could tell that it was exactly the same as I remembered it. It seemed to me, like most of the mainstays, to be untouched by time. I pulled into the parking lot of the Best Western Hotel and Restaurant across the street so I could just sit and look at the place for a while.

It was a good old-fashioned car wash where two guys would scrub down those hard to clean places along the bottom of the car and scrub down both bumpers before a roller would pop up and push the car through the actual building. Then the twirling brushes of the wash area, the jetting streams of the rinse cycle and the giant blow dryer at the end would not only clean their car but also treat the customer to quite a spectacular ride.

About a hundred feet from the wash building was the canopy covering three gas pump islands. On the center island, which was full service, was a little building where the two other attendants waited on gas customers and sold wash tickets.

This was definitely the coolest place in town for a boy to work. It stirred memories and emotions inside of me like no other place in town. It was the first job I had ever enjoyed and I met a lot of friends there but it was more than that, it was the starting point of the most exciting adventure in which I have ever been involved, stemming from the most incredible story that I have ever heard.

Suddenly I became aware of the fact that I had been sitting there for quite a while letting the memories lure me into a dreamlike trance. Realizing this, I pulled back onto Main Street and headed out of town toward home.

I would be later now than I had told my mom I would be. This would mean that she's already called the State Troopers and Sheriff's Department wanting to know if there had been any fatal accidents along the interstate today. I would just have to disappoint her. I often joked that getting killed in a car wreck my mom could forgive but being an hour late was something for which she had little tolerance.

As I neared the dirt road that led to my parent's house, I began to go over some things in my mind that I knew were inevitably for this weekend. My dad will want to play a friendly game of cards that will lead to him telling me how much more money he makes with his truck farming business than I make with my job, quickly followed by the suggestion that I move back here where I belong and work with him. My only defense here is to stay significantly ahead of him during the game so that his concentration remains on the cards.

My dad really hates to lose at anything so winning the card game will buy me some time until dinner when he'll bring up the subject again.

My mom, bless her heart, will then come to my rescue. Even though I'm 33 years old now and can quite aptly take care of myself, I guess old habits are hard to break. This will lead to the two of them arguing at the top of their lungs about everything from letting me run my own life to who shot Kennedy.

Now, being out of the loop, I can just walk away and go watch television if I want. I'll just have to turn the volume up to hear it.

Then there will be the visit to Granny's. She lives in a small wooden house, which she keeps at about 80 degrees at all times, on the same dirt road about 300 yards from Mom and Dad. Granny, who is my mom's mother, is 87 years old and still deep fries everything in two inches of lard. I can't tell her chicken from her pork chops. The strange thing is, I think she is in better shape than anyone else in the family. She'll hug me tight and tell me how good it is to see me, followed by comments on how fat I've gotten, ultimately leading to inquiries about why I don't have a cook. That's Granny lingo for "Why aren't you married?"

Granny is quite a character. Not all of her grandchildren go out of their way to spend time with her because she can be quite belligerent and cusses like a sailor. She has her few favorites, however, that she utilizes for different things. My cousin, Tom, who is two years older than me, bless his heart, is her handyman. No matter what she needs done, be it home repairs or auto work, he gets stuck with those responsibilities. I know that he must be a whiz mechanic just to keep her car going.

She's had the same car for many years although she only drives back and forth out the dirt road. It's not safe for her to drive on the highway anymore. One day I came home to visit and I noticed her old '63 Impala seemed to be a much darker shade of blue than I remembered.

When I mentioned this to Mom, she told me that Granny had painted it. I couldn't believe she would dish out money for something cosmetic; it wasn't her style.

When I went out to see her that day and got nearer to the vehicle, it became clear that she had not spent money to have it painted, she had done it herself. You could still see the brush strokes.

My role was strictly entertainment. Every time I came home, I would usually take her out to eat or even to go fishing if the weather was good. She loves to fish, although her reflexes are not what they used to be and actually getting the line out in the water and not hitting me with it has become challenging. I actually find her to be very funny but have been embarrassed a few times, myself.

For example, once I took her to the grocery store and as we were checking out, a bag boy began to bag the groceries. He was only about 17 or so and he was a little on the heavy side and it wasn't muscular in any sense of the word.

Granny, who apparently never learned to whisper, looked at me and said, "I didn't know they let girls be bag boys."

"Granny!" I said, my face turning red, "That's a boy."

"Well, hell fire, he's got titties like a girl."

Ah, home sweet home. If I ever start to wonder why I don't live here anymore, it only takes one visit to figure it out again.

At the end of the dirt road was the small thirty acre farm where I had lived my entire youth. Half of the land had been cleared for farming while the other half remained full of pine, oak, and hickory trees with a creek running through the middle. It was indeed a great place to grow up far from the worries and crimes of the city.

I had often thought if I did one day get married, this would be where I would want to raise my family.

The land had been given to my mom from my granddad and when I was about four years old, our dad, with the help of my mom's brother, had built a small wood frame house at the front end of the property for us to live in.

My dad was quite the carpenter. He knew a magic word and if you know this word, you will never need a tape measure, a level, or a square—ever. That word is "closeternuff."

Let me give you an example. Once my uncle yelled out that he needed a two-by-four and he needed it to be cut 23 ¼ inches long.

Trying to be helpful, I brought Dad the tape measure.

"I'll just eyeball it," he smiled.

I stood there holding the tape measure as my dad used his incredible visual skills to determine where to cut the board. He then held it up and said, "closternuff."

After a few months the house was built, or semi-built to be more accurate. Dad decided we could go ahead and move in and he would finish the little things like the ceilings and interior walls afterwards. This was of course never done by the time Mom and Dad finished building a new house 26 years later.

Dad had actually started building the new house 17 years earlier which provided a good excuse to not complete the one we were in.

Most times, back in the days of the old house, we didn't have electricity so we relied on kerosene lamps for light and an old Ashley wood burning stove for heat. Water for drinking, bathing, and cooking was retrieved from a spring down in a hollow about 200 feet from the house.

Carrying four empty gallon jugs down and filling them with water to bring back to the house was just one of the chores I remember from my childhood. Others included chopping wood with an axe and feeding the hogs.

"Where have you been?" Mom snapped as I opened the door leading from the garage of the new house to the kitchen. "Do you know that I've been worried sick? I even called the Sheriff's Department thinking you might have been in a wreck."

I couldn't help but smile.

Her demeanor quickly changed; however, as she hugged me and told me how glad she was to see me.

Mom was now 56 years old and her hair was getting a little gray around the edges. She was all of 4 feel, eleven inches tall with a little padding forming around her mid-section. She still wore glasses and had always done so since I could remember, although the style had changed many times over the years. She still prepared home cooked meals every night of the week, even after putting in her long hours boarding socks at one of the mills. I still think she's the hardest working person I've ever known.

"Supper will be ready in a few minutes so put your things away and get ready."

Walking into the living room I came across an all too familiar scene. It was my dad wearing no shirt, sitting in his recliner, and watching a ball game. He was sporting the darkest, deepest, brownish-red tan I had ever seen. Of course it was only from his neck up and from the middle of each of his biceps down. The rest of his torso was as white as a sheet.

Dad stood about five feet, nine inches and still displayed the remains of what used to be a very muscular body. He still had big shoulders and arms but it was now combined with a large belly which protruded outward a good ways as he sat in his chair.

Looking back on my youth, I have few memories of him wearing a shirt around the house.

He had been in the army when he was younger and often bragged of his undefeated boxing years. Although Dad had a tendency to exaggerate, I never really doubted this story because he was still the fastest and strongest man I have ever known. I could currently bench press 450 pounds yet he could toss me around like a rag doll.

His strength was matched only by his speed which was borderline super-heroic. He could outrun most people, believe it or not, while running backwards and letting them run normally. He said he had gotten it from his father. I believed this also because older people on the mountain still told folklore legends about the speed and agility of my grandfather.

Dad grew tomatoes and okra every year and sometimes corn and watermelons. He utilized our land but also rented land for crops. He would take them to the Curb Market in Chattanooga, Tennessee to sell and make pretty good money doing so.

Without so much as a hello, my dad starts talking to me about crops, the weather, and other farmers in the area as if I had never left home. He begins to mention names and events as if I have a clue to what he's talking about.

It's like catching the last fifteen minutes of a two-hour movie. Luckily, they're rhetorical stories that require no feedback and you're fine as long as you maintain eye contact and nod occasionally.

"Hey," Dad said, looking up quickly, his eyes shining as if he had thought of a cure for cancer. "How about a game of cards before supper?"

"Too late," Mom yelled from the kitchen, saving me yet again. "Supper's ready so go get washed up."

The rest of the evening went pretty much as expected. In fact, they were still arguing when I decided to turn in. It had been a long drive and I was pretty tired.

As I sat on the edge of the bed looking around the room that had belonged to my little brother, who was now serving in the Marine Corps, I realized that he had decorated it with a lot of things from my old bedroom in the old house. The same old Bruce Lee posters adorned the walls and the same H.G. Wells paperback books were in the little bookcase compartment on the headboard of the same bed I used to sleep in.

I fumbled through the volumes until I found my favorite, The Time Machine. I pulled it out and was thumbing through the pages when there was a knock on the door whereupon my mom entered carrying some newspaper clippings and what appeared to be an old shoe box.

Mom was notorious for saving every newspaper article that involved anyone I might have known in the past. She'd clip them out of the paper and save them until I came home to visit. I guess she was afraid of someone I knew getting married, getting divorced, having a baby, or getting killed without me knowing about it.

She handed me the clippings and placed the shoe box on the bed. I looked at the first one which read, MICHAEL THOMAS CATCHES PIRANHA IN TENNESSEE RIVER.

That headline was interesting, especially since he caught it in the same place where I used to swim.

"That's pretty scary," I said, holding the picture up to the light. "You never know what people will throw into the river these days."

"I thought you'd be interested in that one," Mom said smiling, "because I remember you went to school with Michael Thomas."

"That's true Mom," I couldn't help but laugh. "But this kid in the article is 18 years old and even though the Michael I went to school with was indeed 18 the last time we saw him, I'm pretty sure that he would have aged like me."

"Okay, wise guy. I was just trying to do something nice for you," she said as she got up to leave.

Mom really wasn't unintelligent by any means, she just didn't always concentrate. Someone in the family could tell a joke just as we were all sitting down for dinner and everyone would laugh except Mom. About twenty minutes later when we were starting on dessert, Mom would start laughing. That's how long it took for the joke to sink in.

"Oh," Mom looked back before closing the door, "I found that shoe box when I was cleaning the basement. I think it's your stuff inside."

I scanned through the rest of the clippings about old friends and whatever this town considered newsworthy and then picked up the shoe box. It was old and faded. I could barely make out the word NIKE on the side. My first thought was that it couldn't be mine remembering that I had never owned a pair of Nikes in high school, much to my disappointment, since they were the "in" thing at the time.

Taking the top off I noticed a stack of pictures, some old letters, and even an old garter from one of several prom dates. Glancing through the pictures, I noticed several with me and some of the guys at the car wash.

I had thought, after seeing the young boys at the car wash earlier today, that no way were we that young when we worked there, but here in my hand was proof. We were kids then. We were young, ignorant, fearless, hopeless kids.

I hadn't seen these pictures in a long time. In fact, I remember thinking they were lost for good. There were several things from that period in my life that I had misplaced, one thing especially, that I would give anything to have again.

"Wait a minute," I thought, dumping the box's contents onto the bed.

It was a long shot at best but as the contents spread across the bedspread, I noticed the short, purple ribbon peeking out from underneath a couple of old concert tickets. I couldn't believe it. The ribbon was faded and beginning to unravel and the shine had long since vanished but there it was in all its glory—the Purple Heart.

It was like being reunited with a long lost friend. As I lay there in bed staring up into the darkness, my imagination was stirring like crazy trying to organize the events of the past that were connected with that medal. It was this medal, this Purple Heart, that's directly linked to the story and adventure I had remembered earlier and was also, in fact, the only physical souvenir I would have to convince myself over the years that it actually happened. Clutching the ribbon in my hand as if to be sure I didn't misplace it again, I lay there in bed with a strange sense of satisfaction.

I had told the story behind the medal several times but now it would be different; now I could add the factor of show- and-tell to better enhance its validity.

Suddenly I felt like a child on Christmas Eve. Even though I was tired, I knew now that I would not soon fall asleep as more and more images became clear in my mind. I remembered everything, every detail, as if it had happened only yesterday.

I went to school at Sylvania High School in Sylvania, Alabama. I looked up the name once and found it meant wooded area and always thought the town was named aptly. The schoolhouse itself basically consisted of a two story building with a gymnasium on one end and the library and lunchroom on the other. Downstairs was elementary and upstairs was high school.

I think a true turning point for me was my senior year. I had not even considered the possibility of going to college because I didn't even think it was something I was allowed to do. I thought college was for rich people or at least the middle class, not for kids who lived on pig farms in small, half-finished shacks with no electricity.

My oldest sister had gotten married and then pregnant her senior year so Dad made her drop out of school and my sister just ahead of me had dropped out because she hated it. Mom was the only one in the family that graduated from high school and she let me know in no uncertain terms that she expected me to do so, also. That was the limit of her expectations, however.

I had come to accept the fact that most teachers tend to look down on students like me for no other reason than being poor. Well, that and I was a real smart aleck. So I never had anyone encouraging me to pursue education beyond high school. When I started playing football, all of the male jock-type teachers started treating me better so I was satisfied with that.

I was pretty good at football, mainly because of growing up the way I did and with the genetics passed on from my dad meant that I was a lot stronger than anyone else on the team and faster than most.

That wasn't the only thing I got from my dad. Dad had only made it to the second grade so obviously school wasn't that important to him, either. That might not be fair to say because it wasn't uncommon in those days for the men to pull their sons out of school to help work on the farms. But Dad was a mathematical genius. He understood numbers so well that I often wondered what higher math functions he was capable of grasping.

Math came easy for me, also, so when it came time for me to take electives in high school, I did what everyone else did; I took classes that required little or no effort to pass. The different was, with me that meant math classes instead of shop or home economics. I had already taken Algebra One, Algebra Two, Pre-Calculus, Analysis, and was taking Calculus my senior year and I was doing this because I didn't even have to study to coast through the class.

There was only one teacher for higher math courses at our little school and that was Mrs. Nester. That meant that I had already had her several times before this class.

Her husband was the science teacher for Sylvania as well..

She asked me one day where I was going to college and was absolutely stunned when I told her I was not.

"What do you mean you're not going?" she snapped.

"What did she mean, 'what do I mean?'" was all I

could think.

"With your understanding of math, you should definitely be continuing your education. What were you planning on doing, then?"

That was a good question. I had not even considered it. I certainly didn't want my dad's life and I hated the mills so I really didn't know.

"I didn't think I could afford to go to college," I said.

She told me about her college days and explained that she was not from a rich family, either. She explained to me about Pell Grants and student loans and work programs until she convinced me that perhaps I was allowed to go to college after all.

It was really a revelation to me that not only was I indeed allowed to go to college, but someone actually cared if I went or not. I started to look into college courses and began to wonder what field I would like to go into. Mrs. Nester had chosen me several times to be her teacher's aid and told me that I might want to consider a degree in math and possibly becoming a math teacher like her.

It was something to think about. I experienced a feeling that I had never experienced before, the feeling that I had a choice about where I wanted my life to go. I had never felt that before.

Early in each school year, Mrs. Nester always held her yearly tryouts for the math team and insisted I try out. I did and was surprised to learn that I had one of the highest scores so I was offered a spot of the math team. I took the spot and started competing in math competitions. Our little school in the wooded area competed against much larger schools. In fact, we were the smallest school to complete but we held our own.

It was quite a strain on me to be on the football team

and on the math team. I was the only one that was on both but Mrs. Nester rescheduled math team practice on opposite days of football practice just for me. That meant that I had football practice on Monday nights and Wednesday nights, math team practice on Tuesday nights and Thursday nights, football games on Friday nights and math competitions on Saturday.

One Saturday we had a competition at Austin High School in Decatur, Alabama. Competitions were made up of two events, the written test which consisted of 40 questions and four tiebreakers and the ciphering event which consisted of one member from each school taking a desk on the auditorium floor and competing against a member from each of the other schools to solve a problem which had been posted up on the projector screen. Points were awarded for the top five fastest times. The teams were made up of four members so the ciphering continued until each player had his turn.

Everyone knew Mrs. Nester's rule on the written test: only answer the ones you know. There was a penalty for guessing which meant you got points counted off for wrong answers the same way you got points added on for correct answers so some students would even finish with negative scores.

For some reason I felt really weird that day. I was really clear-headed and ready for this competition. I'd had days like that in sports when I was really up for the game and played beyond my ability but this was the first time I had ever experienced this on a mental level.

I began to take the written test and everything seemed so clear.

Afterwards, Mrs. Nester started asking everyone how many they answered. The average was around 15. When I told her I answered all of them, she freaked out.

"You know better," she said.

"I think I did well," I replied.

I was right. I took first place. In fact, my score was so high it elevated the entire team to first place so we went home with two first place trophies that day. The math team had never placed in the top three before so this was quite a day.

All of the teachers treated me differently after that day and Mrs. Nester made it her personal task to make sure I went to college. She helped me apply for grants and helped with the admissions applications until I was set.

I was confident now as well. I knew that my life would now move in a new direction and that this chain of events would in turn lead to other events and the chain reaction would take over from there. The road ahead of me was paved with opportunity. Of course, I needed transportation to get down it.

After football season had ended my senior year, I went to work in a hosiery mill working the night shift to save up enough money to put down on a car. I was a knitter which meant I ran about 20 knitting machines that spun the yarn into toeless socks. My job was to take the socks that the machine spits out, pull them up on my left arm to inspect them and make sure there were no runs or loose thread, turn the sock inside out, and lay them in stacks and bundle them in groups of 24 to be placed into a box and sent to the seaming department.

You could always tell a knitter because they had no hair on their arm, their left arm for right handed people, beginning below the elbow and running to the hand.

What made this really tough on me, other than standing eight hours every night, was because the night shift was from ten o'clock at night until 6 o'clock in the morning. This meant that I would have to leave work in Fort Payne and drive directly to school in Sylvania which was located on the mountain. This is before schools instituted any kind of work programs so I attended school until 3:30 in the afternoon where I would then drive home and do any homework I needed to do, crash for a few hours, and then get up to go to work again.

For the rest of my senior year, I was basically a zombie. I did this right up until graduation and although my boss said I could come back anytime I wanted, I vowed that I would never go to work in a hosiery mill again. Although I admired my mom and other people who can go to work every day putting in that daily grind in the mills, this is one vow that I'm glad I've kept.

Most jobs in hosiery mills involve you sitting or standing in one place for eight hours doing the same thing over and over and since most of the jobs are based on production work, you really don't have time to do anything but hustle the entire time working as fast as you can. This is how you bring home a decent paycheck.

It had served its purpose, however, and I had bought a 1974 Chevrolet Monte Carlo. It wasn't anything spectacular, but your first car, like your first love, holds a special place in your heart. And I really loved that car.

I was a greenish gray in color with a red, half landau top. It had a red, velour interior with captain bucket seats. It had wagon wheel style mags with Goodyear radials. It also still had an eight track tape player which got a lot of laughs from my friends.

Of course you could still buy eight track tapes in 1983 so I did that until I saved enough money to replace it with a cassette deck.

It was a solid running automobile with a 350 chevy engine that got me back and forth to work and school but would later stand up to a greater challenge when it would take me and a crazy old Vietnam veteran halfway across the country.

But that's later.

My payments were $74 a month for the car and, fortunately, I had paid up several months before quitting work.

I graduated from Sylvania High School in May of 1983.

The fall after graduation I enrolled at Northeast State Jr. College, a two year prep-college which was located only about twelve miles from home. It was a good way to test the waters of the real world without having to jump into the deep end. I had planned, like a lot of other students from the area, to go to Northeast for at least a year before moving on to a major university. You could take care of all your preliminary courses here and hopefully boost your grade point average before going on to the more serious classes pertaining to your major. In fact, you could go to Northeast for the entire two years without having to declare a major. It was less expensive, your credits transferred easily, and most importantly, you could save on the rent, food, and utility bills by living at home with Mom and Dad.

This concept was a little more appealing at this point in my life.

As the fall quarter progressed, however, my car payments were about to be due again and I was having trouble finding a job that worked around my college schedule. This was probably the closest I ever came to breaking my vow because living in my dad's house and not having a job meant one thing—helping him work the farm.

In the fall and winter when he wasn't farming, he was cutting firewood and pulp wood to sell. Pulp wood consists of pine trees cut into eight feet lengths which we would load onto a two ton truck which had been converted for this purpose.

Converted means that the bed had been removed and four long metal poles were welded to each corner of the frame and sticking upwards about six feet high. The wood was then laid right across the frame until the encasement was completely full. Then we would drive the wood down to the lumber yard where they purchased the pine trees which were then sent to paper mills to be converted into paper.

As winter approached, he normally switched to firewood which was more profitable and a whole lot easier to handle. It just involved more cutting and we only used oak and hickory.

As long as you had a job and were bringing home a paycheck, Dad was content to hire other people to help him. But no job meant there was no excuse. Living under his roof meant you had to abide by his rules. This meant working for him and your payment was getting to live under his roof. Going to college would not get you off the hook either because simply put, going to college did not produce a paycheck. This made looking for a real job priority one because I'll assure you, running a chainsaw and loading wood for several hours a day made working in the mills seem not so bad after all.

Meanwhile, college life was moving right along with everyone feeling out the new environment and getting to know new classmates. It really was a whole different world from high school. Instructors were less personable but they were less demanding as well. There was no dress code like in high school and no attendance call. I guess the instructors and professors figured it was your money you're spending now, so it was up to you to be in class so you could pass.

There were several of my classmates from Sylvania and a lot of people I had played sports with from other schools on the mountain. There were a lot of people from Fort Payne

High School, also, but I didn't really know any of them.

After a few weeks, however, I met a guy from Fort Payne and we hit it off right away. His name was Steven Stoner, and like myself, had been somewhat of a jock in high school. He had been a pretty good football player but had excelled in wrestling. He would always tell me what a good wrestler I would have been but, unfortunately, the small school that I went to didn't offer it.

Steven was only about an inch taller than me with almost the same build. He had dark brown hair with blue eyes. I guess he was fairly attractive but that's not how he saw himself. To Steven, Steven was the hottest male commodity at Northeast State Junior College and didn't mind telling you this. He really thought every girl in college wanted him.

Other than being God's gift to women, however, he did have a great sense of humor and was a genuine friendly guy so we got along just fine.

"What are you doing after school?" I asked Steven one day, figuring it was time to expand our friendship past the confines of the University.

"I have to go to work," he replied. "I work at the Shell Car Wash in town."

It turns out Steven had worked at the car wash since he was in the ninth grade. He went on to the University of Alabama after a couple of years at Northeast and then returned to Fort Payne to work for the same company that owns the car wash. It is the only place to this day that he's ever worked and right now is an executive with the company.

"We need some help there if you're interested in a job."

A Job? Did I hear him correctly? Had the fates been listening? He had no idea what that statement meant to me. That was like asking a man who just walked through a desert if he wanted a drink. I dared to wonder if this was finally a chance to get out of the wood cutting business or the okra picking industry.

Before I could even say that I had been looking for a job and that sounded like a great idea, he continued, "Why don't you come down today and talk with Skip. He's the manager of the car wash. He's a crazy Cajun but fun to work with. If he likes you, he'll hire you."

I remember thinking that Steven was probably exaggerating just a bit and that surely this fellow Skip would look for more qualifications on which to base employment. Nevertheless, a window of opportunity had opened and I was not about to pass up the possibility of expanding my experiences past the pain staking production work of the mills or the pain inducing labor of the farm.

Driving home from school that day found me with mixed emotions: excitement about the prospect of real employment coupled with the fear of telling my dad about it. It wasn't that he would get angry and try to lay down the law or anything like that. My dad wasn't that way. He would just shake his head and say okay, but deep down you could tell he was disappointed. He couldn't understand why someone, even a young person, wouldn't be satisfied with a convenient job like working in the family farming business. Sure, he knew it was hard, dirty work, but by definition, that's what work was. Having a career or even enjoying your job were concepts of which he had never been introduced.

I had to find my own niche in the world, though, so after a short, somber conversation, I left my dad in the woods that afternoon and headed for town.

As I walked into the office of the car wash that afternoon, Skip was reprimanding two of the employees pretty hard for spending too much time on the phone. I would learn later that this was his pet peeve, which made it incredibly easy to get into trouble, because, as I would find out, girls love to call the boys working at the car wash.

Skip Jones was all of five foot, six inches tall, in his early thirties I was guessing, stocky built with glowing red cheeks. He had large front teeth which stuck out a little, and straight, sandy-brown hair which he kept neatly parted on one side. He had graduated from Louisiana State University with a business degree and had probably taken this job just until he could find real employment. He did indeed have a thick Cajun accent and you could tell he was the kind of person that loved to laugh for even though he was chastising these boys quite firmly, he couldn't help but throw in a joke here and there.

The jokes didn't make the boys laugh, however, nor were they intended to, but were strictly for his own benefit. These two poor guys were just standing there like stone fearing for their jobs and Skip was making jokes at their expense to amuse himself.

He had the oddest laugh I had ever heard. I can still here it plainly in my mind but can think of no way to describe it except to say that instead of the traditional 'ha' sound, it seemed more to start with the letter 'G.'

Dismissing the two boys, he looked up at me and asked, "What can I do for you?"

"Uh, my name is Leo. I go to college with Steven. He told me that you might be needing some help here."

I suddenly realized that I wasn't really prepared for this job interview.

"Leo," he said, closing one eye and staring up toward the ceiling as if trying to figure out from where he knew me. "Oh yeah, Leo. You go to college with Steven. He told me about you."

Skip was good. He actually had me thinking that Steven

had already paved the road for me when in fact I found out later that he hadn't even mentioned that I might be coming by today.

He went on with the facade, "Steven has told me a lot about you. You're the one that has the drinking and drug problem."

He was so serious and said that so matter-of-fact like, you would think he was reading it right off my resume. This really caught me off guard and my initial thought was to correct him and clear my good name, but something about the way he was staring at me made me wait. It was as if he was searching for, or expecting, a dumbfounded response in defense of these absurd allegations so he could get a good laugh out of my gullibility.

As I stood fast, expressionless, he continued in my silence.

"So you'll probably come to work drunk all the time and try to sell drugs to all my employees. Is that it?"

Now it was appearing more and more like a set-up.

"No, sir," I replied, gambling that I was judging his character correctly. "I'll wait till I get to work to start drinking and I'll only sell drugs to the customers."

My instincts were accurate. Skip laughed so hard he almost fell out of his chair. His laughter was so contagious that he had me laughing at myself.

Finally, after what seemed like a very long time to laugh, he managed to regain his composure and wipe the tears from his eyes. He sat and stared at me for several seconds and then the manager of the Shell Car Wash got out of his chair, stuck out his hand, and said, "You're hired."

The cool breezes offered up in the autumn air were a refreshing change from the heat of the summer.

Things seemed pretty good. I was going to college and working at a great place doing fun work and meeting lots of new friends.

I must admit that I looked quite cool in my new Shell Car Wash uniform. Actually, it was only brown Dickey work pants, dark green rubber boots and a khaki work shirt with the Shell emblem sewn on one side and my name on the other side but it may as well have been an Atlanta Braves uniform.

Working at the car wash was a blast. All new employees started out at the wash building prepping cars. You stayed here for at least a month before getting to work at the gas pump area. First you would direct the driver of the car into the track, take their ticket, hand them a damp cloth for their dash and ask them to keep their vehicle in neutral. Then you would take your long handled brush, which would be kept in buckets of soapy water, and wash their windshield, side and rear glass, front of the car, and the bottom panels along the bottom of the car that got really dirty.

I remember Skip telling me that the car should be clean before it ever goes through the wash area and all that the stuff inside really did was give the customer a show convincing them that they got their money's worth.

Then you would flip a switch that would allow a chain driven roller to pop up and push the car through the wash. We always let two rollers pop up to protect the car going through because it never failed that there were always some drivers who could not comprehend the "leave it in neutral" concept and believed the faster they drove through the car wash, the cleaner their car got.

The hours at the car wash were split into two shifts, seven in the morning until two in the afternoon and from then until nine at night for those of us attending school. I did get to work the morning shift occasionally on the weekends but the evening shift was where the action was.

Everybody cruising up and down the strip always stopped in at the car wash to give you the lowdown on what was happening around town. We received tidbits like where the parties were, what guys were dating what girls, which girls weren't dating anyone, and other valuable information like that. It was hub central for teenagers and if they weren't stopping in, they were calling on the phone.

Girls were always calling for a friend of theirs to find out if a guy working at the wash was dating anyone, and if not, was he interesting in dating someone. It wasn't exactly like being in a band, but something about working at the car wash made you somehow more attractive to the girls.

This was a new experience for me, so when a girl called, work or no work, it was hard to get off the phone. This was dangerous because some nights Skip would call the wash just to catch people using the phone. Busy signal after busy signal after busy signal, he would continually call keeping tabs on how much company time you were spending on a personal call, and then the following day, let you know about it in a hell-bent, job-threatening, ass-chewing confrontation.

Other than the occasional run-in with Skip, work was a walk in the park. Only when it got near closing time did you have any real work to do. Both the gas pump crew and the car wash crew had a list of things that had to be done every night before they left.

The gas pump crew's list consisted mostly of paperwork and counting money whereas the wash crew's list consisted of all the dirty stuff like emptying the trash cans, hosing down the wash area, and everybody's least favorite—greasing the midder curtain.

The midder curtain was located in the middle of the wash building and consisted of long strips of material hanging down almost to the floor of the wash. These strips zigzagged back and forth to wash the cars. It had twenty-seven grease fittings and the only way to reach then was to climb up on top of the thing. The worst part about it was when a car pulled up to get washed, you had to just ride it out on top of this moving contraption until the wash was over.

More often than not, the people in the car would look up and notice you in this awkward crouched position hanging on like a monkey and start pointing and laughing. About the only ones that didn't notice you were the ones busy making out, and there seemed to be a lot of those,

No one volunteered for the midder curtain duties so it usually came down to flipping a coin or something along those lines. I developed a plan early on that most nights got me out of it. I would either offer to have a foot race with the slimmer kids or arm wrestle the larger ones.

My Grandfather's speed had been passed along to my father and some of that had filtered down to me. We all had flat feet, also, which made it even more amazing.

One coworker after the other fell for my challenge as I would always see the look on their face as they wondered how this short guy was able to outrun them. If you were to take a look at me, speed wouldn't be the first thing that came to your mind because my legs were not proportional to the rest of me.

I had only become aware of this a year earlier. An artist in high school had drawn some cartoon pictures of members of the football team. They were flattering pictures showing us more muscular than we really were. Mine, however, had very short legs and a long torso. When I asked him why he had drawn me this way, everyone looked at me like I was crazy. They explained to me that the picture was accurate.

Ironically, about a week later I had watched as Burt Reynolds appeared on the Tonight Show with Johnny Carson. He talked about his legs being too short for his body. I remember him joking about someone else walking around with his legs.

I finally realized that I had the torso of someone 5'10", which would make sense because that was about my dad's height, and the legs of someone 5'2", which is why I ended up at a measly five feet, six inches tall.

It worked, however,since people were very willing to take the speed challenge.

Only one coworker ever beat me. His name was Alvin Burt and he looked surprised when I challenged him to a race. A smile came across his face and his eyes opened wide as he eagerly agreed. I finally saw what others had been seeing as I watched him from behind as he crossed the finish line. As it turned out, Alvin had set several records for the track team at Fort Payne High School.

Arm wrestling, however, was no contest, as I easily beat everyone. I had been competing since I was 15 years old and had the combination of technique and strength for this event. I also had several first place trophies.

I tried to teach people that arm wrestling was won by wrist strength, not arm strength. When the competition starts, I don't try to pull the other guy's arm down, I simply twist my wrist. Once I twist my wrist, my opponents hand is now only a few inches from the table and then it's only a matter of time depending on his endurance.

That's the way it went. That's how I usually got the easier duties on the closing list.

After finishing the list one night, I locked up the wash building and waited outside the office with the other wash attendant for the two gas pump attendants to finish their paperwork. This was the system. Everybody hung around until the money was counted and then we all left at the same time to go home while one guy would stop off at the bank to make a night deposit.

We parked our cars at the far end of the lot near the giant vacuums to keep them out of the way of the customers. As we walked to our cars that night making small talk, I noticed a car parked behind the wash building in the alley between the car wash and the chain link fence that separated the parking lot from a grassy ditch leading up to the train track.

It was an older model Buick that appeared to be a two tone brown color. Getting out of the car was what appeared to be a very old man with a white plastic milk jug.

"Who's that?" I asked, throwing out the question to either of them who might have the answer.

"That's Peg, the old bum who's always getting water here," Brian said.

Brian Manning was a senior at Fort Payne High School and one of the gas pump attendants who had been working at the car wash for several months now, a veteran by car wash standards.

"He's too late tonight, though," he added with a laugh. It was a cold laugh that expressed the fact that he was glad he wasn't getting any water.

"Peg?" I thought. "What kind of name is that for a man?"

As the other guys drove off, I stood there a while watching the old man trying to get water from this outside faucet. I knew he would not be successful because I had cut off all the water to the entire facility before locking up, which included this faucet. He kept turning the round handle left and then right as if he couldn't figure out why no water was coming out and maybe there was a secret combination to the handle that would make the water appear.

Thinking that he might need some water for his car, I got into my Monte Carlo and pulled right up behind him in the alley.

I noticed then that his car was a medium brown color and the darker places were actually rusted areas.

Paying me no attention as I got out of my car, the old man was leaning up against the side of the building with his legs wide apart as if he were balancing himself. He was concentrating solely on the task at hand. Back and forth he turned the faucet handle becoming seemingly disgusted with it and mumbling under his breath the whole time.

He was a pretty good sized fellow with a bit of a mid-section. He was dressed in very old clothes and he looked really rough. He looked as if he hadn't shaved in many weeks as the long, white stubble extended all the way down his neck into his shirt. His long, thin hair was pure white and looked like it hadn't seen a comb in years. I began to wonder if he was drunk because of his appearance and the fact that he seemed to be having trouble standing, relying more on the wall than his own abilities.

"You need some help?" I asked.

He turned around and looked at me as if he didn't understand what I was asking and without so much as a word, returned to his quest for water.

From my headlights I could see inside his car and noticed it was full of clothes, boxes and junk. On his dash I noticed several Styrofoam cups and that's when it dawned on me that he wasn't getting water for his car, he was getting water to drink.

Suddenly I felt very bad for the old fellow. I've always had this soft spot in my heart for people who don't seem to have much in life and to this day I haven't figured out if that is a character strength or a character weakness.

Walking back around to the front of the building, I took out my keys, unlocked the door to the wash, and went in and turned the water back on. As I stood there in the semi-darkness, I imagined the old man filling up the jug and stayed until I was sure he had enough time to do so.

Turning the water back off and locking the door again, I walked around to the alley to find the old man gone.

Oh well, I guess he had too much to do to stay around and thank me.

As I headed toward home that night, I saw the old man sitting in his car in an empty parking lot. It seemed like a familiar sight and I begin to wonder how many times I had seen him before without really noticing him.

It's amazing how your mind can block out certain things, but once you've become consciously aware of something, you will begin to notice it all the time. Such was the case with that old man. After that night, I began to see him all the time.

The next day at work was a typical weekday with business slowing down after four o'clock in the afternoon. After the rush from the mills letting out, only an occasional car would pull up for a wash so we generally goofed off for a while.

Skip was telling a joke upon which he laughed more than we did. There were three car wash employees standing around him providing him an audience. He was a really good guy who didn't make us do something just to earn our pay. If the traffic was slow, he had no problem letting us catch our breath and relax for a while.

I looked up and noticed the old Buick chugging up Main Street leaving a noticeable white trail behind it. It sounded as if it was in dire need of a tune-up and the emissions appeared to be of the ozone destroying level.

I pointed to the car as it went by and said, "Hey, Skip. I saw that old man trying to get water here last night after we had closed up."

It wasn't that I thought that information was newsworthy, I was just fishing for some feedback that might shed some light on the old fellow.

"Yeah, he's always stopping in here to get water or gas," Skip said. "I'll tell you one thing, Jack doesn't like him getting water here."

Jack Freeman was the owner of the car wash and like most rich people I've met in my life, was quite particular about someone getting something from them for free. If he pulled into the car wash while we were all standing around, you would have seen a mad dash by everyone to find something to do.

I met him my very first day on the job. He pulled up to the wash area in a dually, which is a pickup truck with four wheels on the back. He got out of the truck and instructed me to grab a brush from one of the buckets and start cleaning his truck.

I noticed that he hadn't been through the pump area where tickets were sold, nor had he handed me a ticket.

"Have you paid for a wash?" I asked.

Ignoring my question, he continued, "The truck won't go through the wash because of the back tires so just wash it down with a brush out here."

Who in the hell did this guy think he was? I wasn't about to wash his truck for him.

Skip suddenly comes out of the office. "Jack. How ya doing?"

He walked over and shook his hand.

"Leo, this is Jack Freeman, the owner of the carwash."

I smiled and nodded and grabbed a brush and started washing the truck.

After Jack left, Skip explained to me that he did that every time he saw a new person working there.

For the time being, however, there was no sign of Jack so no need to act busy.

As I watched the Buick drive out of sight, Skip asked, "You didn't let him get any water, did you?"

He was smiling as if he knew the answer but wanted to know if I'd admit it.

I offered this answer: "Well, you never know when one of these bums may be a millionaire in disguise trying to find someone worthy to leave their fortune to."

This brought a grin to Skip's face. I'm not sure if he was grinning at the ridiculous possibility of my theory or if he was grinning at my ability to answer a question without actually answering it.

Work went on that evening and I forgot about the old man until about 8:30 that night when I noticed his car at the gas pumps. I watched as he pumped his gas and then walked over to the little building to pay.

He walked with the aid of a cane and not very well even then. He slowly made his way over and paid for his gas and then slowly walked back to his car. Getting into his car, he pulled away from the pump islands, drove straight by me, and pulled back into the alley again.

Curious, I walked over to the corner of the wash building so I could see down the alleyway and, just like the night before, he stopped right beside the water faucet and got out of his car with his jug.

This time the water had not been turned off and he was successful in filling his jug with no problem. He took the jug of water and put it in his back seat and, with a little bit of struggling, negotiating himself back behind the wheel. He shut the car door and just sat there.

His car was running so I assumed he wasn't having any trouble but he wasn't going anywhere. I begin to think he was going to park there for the night when I noticed his reflection in the side-view mirror.

He was staring directly at me. I felt chills running down my spine and I started to walk away but then he raised his left hand ever so slightly and drove off.

I smiled as I thought to myself, "Perhaps he had time to say thank you after all."

"She wants me," Steven said as the car drove away carrying a very pretty girl who had just gotten gas.

After getting promoted to pump attendant, this became a phrase that I would hear several times a night while working with Steven. The sad part was, Steven really believed it. We were a good pair, though, and I enjoyed working with him because he did seem to know everybody in town.

One night as it was getting near closing time, I noticed the old rusted Buick chugging up to the gas pumps. I felt sort of strange realizing that this would be the first time to see the old man at close range.

"Right on time," I heard Steven say.

Turning around I noticed him staring out the window at the old Buick. He looked back at me smiling, "Old Peg's here to get his seventy-five cents worth of gas."

I started to ask Steven about the old fellow when I heard him hang up the nozzle. I watched him use his cane to walk over to the cashier window.

As he got near the window, I noticed that he wasn't as old as I had thought him to be. It was just the long white hair, unshaven look and the cane that gave him the appearance of being older.

As he glanced up, I could see the recognition in his

eyes finding me there for the first time but he said nothing.

"How are you doing tonight?" I asked.

"Seventy-five cents," was his only reply, holding out his hand and dumping three quarters into mine.

He turned, walked back to his car and drove away. Before the car even pulled onto Main Street, Steven was having a good laugh at my expense.

"How's it going tonight," he laughed mockingly. "Boy, you two sure hit it off well."

"How did you know how much gas he was going to get?" I asked out of sincere curiosity while trying to change the subject at the same time.

"That's how much he always gets," he replied.

Okay. I could tell he had it down to a science.

Less than an hour later as we were getting ready to close for the night, I was still thinking about the old fellow.

"Why do you call that old man Peg?" I asked Steven.

"Because he has two peg legs," Steven replied with a 'what a stupid question' look on his face.

"You don't even know his real name, then?" I asked.

"Nope. But I do know what happened to him."

Noticing the obvious interest in my facial expression, Steven continued. He used to be this famous radio disc jockey."

It's strange now, but I remember thinking at that moment that he must have been quite a celebrity if he was a DJ. I guess growing up in a town with no local television station, a radio personality was the pinnacle of local stardom.

"Well, he was messing around with this married woman and one night while they were parking, this car pulls up behind them with the lights on bright. Peg gets out of the car and walks between the two cars trying to see who's in the other car. Turns out, it was her husband and he floors the gas pedal and rams Peg, pinning him between the two cars. That's how he lost his legs. After that he just lost all contact with everyone and started living out of his car. He has a sister here in town but he doesn't have anything to do with her, either."

You could tell that Steven was enjoying telling the story. It was the joy of being able to display the insight that other people may lack, much the same, I imagined, as the person who got to tell him. The sad part is, much like Steven, I took it to be the gospel. But it would help fill a void in my curiosity at least until I would learn the truth.

"What are you doing Friday night after we get off work?" Steven asked.

"Don't know. Why?"

"Why don't you come over to my house," he continued. "I'm having some guys over to watch a movie."

"Sounds good," I replied.

Actually, I wasn't sure how good it sounded. I liked Steven and had been to his house several times, but his mom scared me a little.

She was divorced, or widowed, I'm not sure which. She was medium build with the same dark wavy hair and blue eyes that Steven had. She had very large breasts and she dressed like a gypsy. The first time we met, after talking with me for five minutes, she told me than my name was perfect because my zodiac sign was Leo also.

"How did you know that?" I asked, somewhat taken aback.

"Leos are easy to spot," she said. "They are sensitive, great conversationalists, and love being the center of attention."

Maybe she really was a gypsy. She also asked if I would let her read my palm.

I said okay so she took my right hand and stared at my palm and told me that I would never get married because my love line didn't cross my life line. She told me a lot of other things as well but the way she was caressing my hand led me to believe that my future was not all she wanted to delve into.

She started buying me things, too. After my first visit, every time I went over there she would have a gift for me. One time it was a nice Polo shirt and she wanted me to try it on right away.

That should have been a red flag, as well as her constant flattering comments on my looks and her little sexual innuendoes.

I kept my word, however, and after work that Friday night I went over to Steven's to watch a movie. There were three other guys there besides me and Steven. I knew two of them from the car wash but didn't recognize the third. Steven's mom was there and she immediately let everyone know that she would be sitting next to me and for them to leave that seat open.

When Steven started calling out the names of the movies for us to choose from, I almost freaked out.

"We have Ecstacy Girls, Peach Fuzz and Debbie Does Dallas."

I wasn't shocked that a group of guys were getting together to watch porn since I'd done that several times with other friends. What shocked me was the fact that apparently his mom was going to be watching with us and was going to be sitting next to me.

As Steven put in the first VHS tape, his mom grabbed the throw pillows off of the sofa and tossed them to all the guys.

"Here, you better keep these in your lap," she laughed.

She tossed me one also so I placed the pillow in my lap

as instructed.

Steven turned off the lights as the movie started and I still felt uncomfortable as his mom took her seat beside me. I couldn't believe I was watching porn with a friend's mom in the same room.

It got worse.

About halfway through the first movie, I felt her hand slowly working its way underneath my pillow. I realized then that this was her intention for the pillow all along. Pretending they were to cover any embarrassing physical metamorphosis that we as young men might experience while watching such movies was purely a distraction.

I was between a rock and a hard place. No pun intended. I sat motionless as her hand made its way all the way to my crotch and began a slow, methodical massage.

Okay, it wasn't terribly horrible. The fact that the television wasn't giving off enough light for anyone to really know what was going on didn't hurt matters.

It was only when she started trying to work the zipper that she had to move her arm in such a way as to give things away. I didn't know what to do so I got up and, keeping the pillow in place, excused myself to the bathroom.

Everyone laughed as I walked away holding the pillow in front of me.

In the bathroom I stared into the mirror and began shaking my head as I wondered what I had gotten myself into. I walked back into the living room and told everyone goodnight.

"You're leaving?" his mom asked

"Yeah, I have to get up early."

"Why don't you come by tomorrow while Steven's at work and we can watch some more movies?" she asked.

I could not believe she said that in front of everyone.

"I have to work, too," was my response.

Steven walked me to the door. "We'll have to do this again sometime."

"I don't know," I replied.

"Yeah," Steven said looking back towards his mom, "I don't know, either."

I walked out to my car and drove away wondering about his last statement. Had he known what was going on? I felt really odd and knew I would feel even more uncomfortable when I saw him at work the next day.

Since it was a Friday night, I decided to make a trip through town after leaving Steven's house to see if anyone was out and about and to give me a chance to clear my head. After circling the south Y, I headed back through town with intentions of driving home for the night. As I passed the car wash, I glanced up in my rear view mirror and noticed the front of the old Buick sitting in the alley alongside the wash building again.

I couldn't believe it. Didn't he know by now what our hours were?

Turning around, I figured I could turn the water on for him one more time but I was going to explain to him first that he needed to get here before we close from now on. As I pulled into the alley, I got a bit of a shock when I noticed that there was a Police car parked behind Peg's car and an officer had his hands resting upon the driver's door leaning over talking with him through the open window.

It was Officer Lane Preston. I didn't know him personally, but I heard plenty of stories about how tough he was. My first inclination was to back up and leave but I figured if he was going to harass Peg for using the outside faucet, the least I could do was defend him by saying we allowed him to do so.

As I got out of my car, Officer Preston looked back at me, probably wondering what the heck I was doing. I was pretty nervous as I started walking toward them but then something happened that took me by surprise. Peg stuck his hand out of the window and Lane Preston extended a firm handshake, backed away from the window and Peg drove away.

He then turned and walked straight toward me.

"Can I help you?" he asked.

"I work here," I blurted out, thinking this would provide the best justification for me being here. "I saw that man's car around here and I thought he was trying to get some water."

"And you figured it was your responsibility to run him off," he grimaced. "I don't know why you kids have to treat people this way. He hasn't done anything to you and I doubt that one jug of water a day is going to break the owner of this place."

One surprise after another.

"No, no, you don't understand," I rushed out. "It's just that he's come here before after we've closed and the water has already been cut off inside so I've went in to turn it back on for him. That's what I thought had happened tonight until I saw you back here and I thought you were giving him a hard time about being here so I was going to tell you that he always gets water here."

As I caught my breath after that explanation, he stood there, squinting, his eyes looking me over as if trying to decide if I was being honest with him.

"I'm Lane Preston," he said, sticking out his hand.

I introduced myself and we began to talk. We talked about the weather, the car wash, football, and finally he started telling me about Peg.

Actually, his name was Jim Terrell and Officer Preston

probably knew him better than anyone else in town. They had attended high school together here in Fort Payne, played football together, and graduated together in 1968. They were also both drafted into the Army shortly thereafter and sent to Vietnam.

"Those were some scary times for me and Jim," he continued. "After we completed training, Jim was hooked up with the 101st Airborne Division and shipped off to God knows where. I don't know where he was in the beginning but he ended up in the worst possible place.

Most of the stuff I saw was after the action.

I was a gunner with a Medevac unit. We would come in with a Huey and our main job was to take badly wounded soldiers from the medic tents back to the hospital units. The bad part about this job was that I never knew what happened to the soldiers after that. I saw so many faces, heard so many prayers that after a few months, the faces all started to run together. "

Officer Preston was no longer making eye contact but staring off into the distance. I could tell that the memories were still strong.

"Did you ever see Jim again over there?" I asked.

"Just once," he said, looking back into my eyes with a stone-cold glare that I could feel penetrating into my soul.

"Just once," he repeated.

Staring back away into the distance, he continued, "I was nearing the end of my tour. It was May 15th, 1969. I remember clearly because it was my birthday. We were in the Huey one day coming back to base when we got a call about a badly shot up group of soldiers in the A Shan Valley. I had just heard about this place a day earlier and I understood it be live with Charlie so we were expecting a hot LZ.

"As we put down near the medic tents, we could still

hear gunfire coming from the hill. I went with the medics because we knew we would need every man to help carry the wounded. We jumped out and ran toward the tents as fast as we could with the other gunner guarding us. Inside the tents were three soldiers wounded pretty badly and a fourth that was dead when we arrived. We grabbed up the four men and carried them to the Huey and lifted off. This was probably the scariest moment for me in the war, waiting on that bird to get airborne again.

"As the medics began to work on the injured men, one of them grabbed my arm and was trying to say something. I put my head down so I could hear what he was trying to say.

"He was saying 'Doc.'

"I tried to explain to him that I wasn't a doctor but everything would be all right. He kept repeating the word 'Doc.'

"I was thinking he was in shock until I heard him say 'Lane.'

"I jerked my head up and looked at his face and it was Jim. He was messed up pretty bad.

"He then started asking about Tommy. 'How's Tommy?' he kept asking.

"I kept asking him who Tommy was and he finally said his whole name, Thomas MacReynolds. I had a sudden bad feeling come over me as I reached over to the dead soldier and pulled out his dog tags. It was him.

"'He's dead Jim,' I told him.

"Jim started crying and muttering over and over, 'He saved us. He saved us.'

"I didn't see Jim again until I got back home. They had taken off both his legs and replaced them with metal limbs. He lived with his sister here in town for many years until she kicked him out. Now he just lives out of his car."

So he did have a sister here in town. Well, at least one part of Steven's story was true.

"Why would his own sister kick him out?" I wondered aloud.

"I wondered that, too," Preston said. "So I went by and asked her. All she would say is that it's his decision. I believe her exact words were, 'He's made his bed, now he has to sleep in it.'

"Deep down though, I kept getting the feeling that it was her husband behind it all because the whole time I spoke with her, he just sat there staring at me."

I just stood there dazed as the story sank in.

"Well, it's late," he concluded, "so you better get on home and thanks for looking after Jim."

"No problem," I replied.

Officer Preston drove out of the alley and I followed him to Main Street where I turned out of town and headed home.

The next morning I went to work and everything seemed fine with Steven. If he did indeed suspect anything from the night before, he never let on.

Over the next few days, I told all the guys at the car wash the story that I had heard and everyone started having a different opinion of Peg after that. As a matter of fact, every-one, including Skip, started calling him Mr. Terrell. A lot of the guys would even pump his gas for him so he didn't have to get out of the car. They would also check his oil, clean his windshield and check the air in his tires. I do believe he was quite confused about what was going on but I think he sensed somehow that I was behind it. He would always give me a look and a slight nod before he left.

The only one that seemed to be bothered was Steven. I guess it made him look pretty silly after telling most of the guys at the car wash his version of what happened. But it was all a front. Deep down I was sure he felt differently about Jim just like the rest of us did and one night I was positive. I saw Steven walking into the alley after Jim had driven back there. I peeked around to watch as Steven took his jug and filled it up for him and waved as he drove away.

Christmas eve, 1983, was the coldest day of my life. I awoke at 6 o'clock and knew it was not a normal day the second I crawled out from under the covers. We didn't have any means of heat in the back bedrooms so I made a mad dash toward the living room.

I immediately opened the flue on the wood heater to allow the air in to start the fire burning again. We would fill up the heater with wood at night and when it was burning very hot, we would shut off the flue and the wood would smolder all night. All you needed to do in the mornings was open the flue and fill it up with wood and you were set.

I grabbed the few pieces of wood that were setting beside the heater and opened the door and threw them in. Nothing was working fast enough that morning, however, and I found myself rubbing my arms to try and stay warm.

As the fire started to roar to life, I began to feel normal again.

I had to run back into my bedroom to get my work uniform but rushed back quickly to dress in the living room. It was a Saturday morning and since Mom was off work, no one else would be up for quite a while.

I dressed for work then filled the heater completely up with wood and left the flue half open. This way it would still be very warm when everyone got up and the wood would not have had time to burn completely out.

As I walked out to my car, I realized that this was no ordinary winter day, especially for Alabama. It was painful, very painful. I began to wish I had come out earlier to start the car and let the heater run for a while but I hadn't thought of it. I got in and cranked the car and turned on the defroster to clear the windshield which was solid ice.

It's common for there to be frost on the windshield. In fact, as long as it's below freezing, with the moisture in the air, there will always be frost. This was more than frost this morning, however, and I became aware that my defroster was not making a dent.

I had never owned an ice scrapper so I started looking around my car for anything that I might could use as a substitute. I noticed a soda bottle in the floor so I took off the cap and got out of the car to try that. It worked well and I was able to clear a spot big enough for me to see so I began the drive to work

I turned on the radio and the weather was the buzz. The DJ was talking about how unusually cold in was and then he gave the temperature and I was taken back. With the wind chill factor, it was 40 degrees below zero.

I arrived at the car wash a few minutes before seven o'clock and Skip was there. He told me that Steven and I would be the only ones working that day and we would be at the pumps. The wash, it turned out, was frozen solid and we couldn't have opened it if we tried.

Steven pulled up a little later and Skip gave him the same news.

Skip then left us there by ourselves and went home. It was an unbelievable day. We started our opening procedures and one thing became apparently clear, neither one of us was wearing enough protection.

We went into the office area at the wash building and scavenged for anything we could find. We made out pretty well coming away with several coats and pairs of gloves for each of us. We also took the heater to add it to our own at the pump island.

The wind was blowing so hard that we had to put concrete blocks in all the trash cans to keep them from blowing away.

When it gets this cold in the South, it is unlike cold weather in the North. The same humidity that make the heat of the summers smothering makes the cold of the winters almost unbearable, even painful, as the moisture in the air penetrates your body clear to the bone.

We were huddled up inside that little booth wearing several coats, several pairs of socks, two pair of gloves, and had two electric heaters going and I still couldn't feel my toes and fingers.

As full service customers pulled up, we would take turns waiting on them, then rush back to the booth as fast as we could.

I'll never forget this one lady pulling up to full service and asking me to put two quarts of Dixie Penn Motor Oil in her car.

Dixie Penn was a recycled oil that only cost one dollar a quart and it was very thick, so most of the people who used it did so because their cars used a lot of oil. Dixie Penn would last longer and was less expensive.

I raised her hood and removed the oil cap and turned up the first quart of oil. Nothing happened. Finally a glob of oil slowly descended to the opening in her valve cover but instead of going in, it just layered back and forth on top.

I called for Steven to come look. He couldn't believe

it.

"It looks like caramel," he laughed.

We literally had to set the two quarts of oil in front on one of the heaters for several minutes to warm them up enough to pour into her car.

We had received word that second shift would be off due to the holiday so we were to close up at two o'clock that afternoon. I could hardly wait. I was ready to get home and bask in the holiday spirit, which means I was ready to start pigging out on Christmas food.

Everyone meets at Mom and Dad's house for Christmas lunch and Mom cooks enough food to feed the Atlanta Falcons. We'll start eating around noon and then the guys will watch football for several hours while we try to digest well more food than our bodies ever intended for us to take in at one time. Then we will put together a little football game in the afternoon and play until dark at which point we'll go back and eat some more.

If there is one actual scale in life that lets you know when you're no longer a kid and have entered the world of adulthood, it would have to be Christmas. When you start looking forward to the food more than the presents, I'd say you've graduated.

I was ready to get home for sure. Unfortunately, my day was long from over.

About 30 minutes before closing time, Jim Terrell started to pull into the pump area of the car wash. He had barely gotten off the road when his car stopped, still about a hundred feet from our booth.

"Uh oh," Steven smirked, "I guess he should get more than seventy-five cents in gas from now on."

I ignored him as I watch Mr. Terrell get out of his car and raise the hood. He apparently was not out of gas. He stood there staring at his motor. It was the blank stare I've seen from other men who have no clue what could be wrong with their car.

He had no coat on at all, just a long sleeve shirt and it wasn't even flannel. After a couple of minutes I couldn't take it anymore and told Steven to watch the pumps while I went see if I could help him.

I walked up beside him and looking only at the motor myself, I asked, "What happened?"

"It just quit," he replied.

This actually constituted the first real conversation we had ever had. I was shocked but I kept my eyes on the motor and continued, "Get in and try it and let's see what it's doing."

He did what I instructed and I listened when he turned the switch over and heard only a clicking noise. It was obvious that his battery was dead. It could have been the cold that drained it or I knew the possibility existed that it might even be the alternator had gone bad.

The only sure way to tell was to get the car started and then you could test it by taking off one of the battery connections while the car is running. If the car continues to run, the alternator is good and the battery is bad. If the car stops, however, the alternator is bad, which is by far the worst case scenario.

As I pulled my car around to boost his car, Steven pulled up in his.

"I've closed up and I'm going to drop off the deposit. Have a merry Christmas."

He quickly pulled away and disappeared down Main Street. I guess he was afraid I was going to ask him to help.

Jim's car started up and I took my jumper cables off and threw them in my car.

Now came the moment of truth. If it was only a dead battery, that was fairly inexpensive and easy to change. I took off one of the battery cables. Of course we would have no such luck. The car died.

He saw the disappointment in my face and asked me what it meant. I explained that he would need a new alternator or the car would never stay running. I knew the alternator itself would cost about $60 and no telling how much for the labor, providing we could find someone to do it on Christmas Eve.

At my request, he rode through town with me and we checked every auto shop I could think of and they were all closed. At least the heater in my car was beginning to thaw me out from being out in the cold so long.

I was ready to throw in the towel until I suddenly remembered that he slept in his car. He would freeze to death if I didn't get his car running.

"Do you have any place you can stay tonight?" I asked. "Maybe with your sister?"

He looked at me like I was crazy, probably wondering how I knew he had a sister. He didn't say anything for several minutes and I began to think that I had really over stepped my boundaries.

Finally, after several minutes of awkward silence, he said, "I'll be fine. Just take me back to my car and I'll wait until after Christmas to get it fixed."

"No way," I thought. "Let me try one more thing," I said, hoping he would agree.

He nodded so I drove to the far south end of town, and to my surprise, the Auto Zone was open.

We walked up to the counter and I told the man that we needed an alternator.

"What make and model car?" he asked.

"71 Buick Riviera," Jim said.

The guy checked his inventory.

"We have one here in stock for that car. It will be $49.95 with a trade in."

"Okay," I replied, "but I'll have to bring you the old one after we get them changed out if that's all right."

"Well, we're getting ready to close in a few minutes."

"Can I bring it back after Christmas, then?" I pleaded.

The man agreed and again, to my surprise, Jim took out a checkbook and wrote the man a check for the alternator. You wouldn't think a man who gives you a handful of change to pay for gas would have a bank account. I had already accepted the possibility that I would have to pay for it but I'm glad I hadn't made a move to do so because I think that might have really insulted him.

Growing up the way I did in the woods on Sand Mountain, made knowing how to replace an alternator a routine job. Shade tree mechanics ran in the family and my cousins next door had the biggest shade tree in the county to work under, a towering Poplar tree with a base diameter of 6 feet that reached a hundred feet into the air with huge limbs positioned just right to mount a chain and hoist to take motors out of cars.

I always kept a toolbox in my trunk so, arriving back at the car wash, I set out to change the alternator in the rusted old Buick.

I asked Jim to wait in my car while I worked to stay warm but he would have none of that and stayed there beside me helping any way he could.

I loosened the alternator enough to slide it forward so I could remove the belt from the pulley. I let the belt just dangle in place. Next came the connectors at the back of the alternator. Even though the battery was pretty dead, I disconnected it as to not have the hot wire spark against the metal mount. I took off the nut that holds the wires that run from the alternator to the switch and unplugged the other wire. I then started to take out the long bolts that hold it in place.

Like most cars, these bolts were in a tiny space so it was tedious getting my fingers in there to work. I finally worked them free and pulled the old alternator out and set it on the concrete beside the car.

I grabbed the new alternator from my car and began the process in reverse.

It was getting near dusk and the weather was either getting colder or my tolerance was getting weaker. You cannot do this kind of work wearing gloves so I had taken them off before I started and now my fingers were so numb that I couldn't tell them apart from the metal on the car.

I began to wonder what the heck I was doing here instead of home in front of a nice fire munching on pecan pie and drinking eggnog. All I had to do was look at Jim standing there wearing that flimsy shirt to answer that question.

It was getting hard to see by the time I finished. I put the old alternator in my car and hooked the jumper cables up one more time and got his car running again. To be safe I checked it again by removing a battery cable and it stayed running this time. I put the jumper cables back in my car, closed my hood and then closed his hood and walked around to his window.

"It's working fine now," I said. "Do you have enough gas to keep it running all night?"

"Yeah," he replied, "I'll be fine now."

Reaching into his pocket he pulled out his checkbook again and asked, "How much do I owe you?"

"No, no," I said shaking my head. "Don't worry about it."

"I can't expect you to do this for nothing. How about fifty dollars?" he persisted.

I declined again and told him it was his Christmas present.

He smiled, stuck out his hand and said, "Thank you, Leo, for everything."

It sounded strange to hear him use my name. For a split second I wondered how he even knew it until I remembered that it was sewn on my shirt. I shook his hand and was about to walk away when I saw the ribbon hanging around the gear shifter with the heart dangling from it.

"Is that your Purple Heart from where you were wounded in Vietnam?" I blurted out before thinking.

"That's it," he said, sliding it off the gear shifter and handing it to me out the window. "Not exactly like winning a gold medal in the Olympics."

I forgot all about the cold as I stood there looking at the medal. "I've never known a war hero."

"Well," he chuckled, "I don't think getting wounded makes you a war hero. I was just in the wrong place at the wrong time. Now Tommy on the other hand, was a true hero."

His eyes took on the same faraway look that I had seen on Officer Preston that night.

"Who's Tommy?" I whispered.

"He's the guy that pulled all three of us out the fire in Vietnam."

He was still staring off into the distance.

As he sat there motionless, the silence allowed my brain to remember that I was freezing to death.

"Tell you what," I said aloud, getting his attention again, "if you really want to pay me somehow, then you can do it by telling me the whole story sometime."

He smiled but before he could say anything, a Sheriff's

car pulled up beside us. A deputy Sheriff rolled down his car window and looked at me and asked, "Are you Leo Whitten?"

"Yes, I am," I replied, somewhat bewildered.

"Call your mom and let her know you're all right so she'll stop calling our office," he said with a grin.

Then he rolled up his window and drove away.

I said goodbye to Jim and drove home.

"Touchdown!" my dad yelled as the Gray team quarterback dove into the end zone for a one-yard score.

The Blue/Gray football game was played every Christmas day at Crampton Bowl, a city owned football stadium in Montgomery, Alabama. It was like the All-star game for college players at the end of the season. A coach was chosen form a Southern team and one from a non-Southern team and they picked players from schools all around the nation that were not going to a bowl game.

Watching the Blue/Gray football game on Christmas day had become as big a ritual as opening presents. At least it was for my dad, my brother-in-law, and me.

The women were busy at this time trying to determine what should be thrown away and what would become leftovers for the next two weeks.

"Extra point good!" Dad continued, holding up his arms like a referee. "We're mounting a comeback."

"Sure Dad," I thought. The Gray was only trailing by 17 points with three minutes to go in the game.

In fact, the Blue had dominated this event since its conception several decades ago.

Dad was a hopeless optimist, however, when it came to this game. He couldn't stand or understand boys from the

North beating good ole Southern boys.

Of course the Blue's players came from all over the nation but the fact that they weren't playing for the Gray team automatically made them a Yankee in my dad's eyes. There were certain teams that he hated more than others such as Norte Dame and Penn State.

I had heard him comment on several occasions that his two favorite college teams were the Auburn Tigers and who-ever was playing Norte Dame.

You would think more rested on the outcome of this game than the first conflict between the Blue and the Gray back in 1861.

As the last seconds of the game wound down, Dad pulled out the little dinner tray beside his recliner. It was obvious he needed a game of cards to vent his frustrations for the game.

Ricky, my brother-in-law, and I pulled up chairs along the makeshift card table and Dad began to deal.

His favorite game was Tunk which was a combination of Rummy and poker.

Dad began with an early lead which got his mind off the football for a while. He then started telling Army and truck driving stories.

I don't know which was worse.

As he started telling about his years in the service, in particular his undefeated amateur boxing career, my mind began to wonder. Mentioning the Army made we think of Jim and I started wondering if he really did have enough gas to last him until tomorrow when the gas stations would be open again.

When the game of cards was over, I got up and told them I needed to go somewhere. I went into the kitchen and put together a plate on ham, turkey, rolls, and potato salad and headed to town.

It was much warmer than it had been yesterday with the temperature reaching all the way up to zero today.

About halfway through town, I noticed the old rusted Buick parked in front of the video store, white puffs of toxins billowing up from the exhaust which immediately comforted me. Jim was smiling as I pulled up alongside of his car as if he was expecting to see me today.

"Merry Christmas," I said as I pulled up beside him.

"Merry Christmas," he echoed.

"Here," I offered as I handed the plate of food out the window. "I thought you might like some good Christmas food."

Jim graciously took the plate and started eating.

Sitting there in silence as he ate, occasionally nodding his approval of the meal, I noticed a gift wrapped package on the seat beside him. Finishing everything on the plate, he took it, along with the napkin and plastic fork I had furnished, and slipped them into a plastic trash bag strung from his cigarette lighter.

"Someone else has already gotten you a present?" I asked, glancing over at the package. "Maybe Santa Claus?"

"Nah. It's from me to my sister. I've been trying to decide if I want to take it to her or not."

"Why is that a hard decision?" I asked, judging that it must be from the look on his face.

"We don't really get along that well anymore," he said. "I was living with her for a while until she got married and I just didn't want to be in their way. She didn't want me to move out but I thought it was best since they were newlyweds and all.

Besides, me and her husband really don't get along. So I've been living out of this here old clunker ever since and she's been pissed at me ever since."

"How can you choose your car over a house?" I questioned.

Jim stared at me with a smile as if he admired my earnestness.

I was serious, too, and I wasn't going to let the subject just be swept away with a smile. "I want an answer," I continued. "I mean, seriously, how long do you think you can go on living in your car?"

"Until May 28th," he replied as simply as if I had asked him an easy math question. "Yep," he repeated, "May 28th."

"May 28th? What's that?" I asked bluntly. "The doctor tell you the exact day that you're going to die?"

Jim just laughed and said, "I'm not dying. At least I don't think I am. Never know though so I guess I should go see my sister. Do you want to drive or ride with me?"

That was a masterful invitation I thought, shaking my head. More and more I became surprised that underneath the rough exterior, an exterior that gave you the impression that this person had no social skills and no wanting to be part of any social structure, lay a deep character with a personality full of memories, laughter and life.

"Come on," I laughed, "I'll drive."

Jim got out of his car carrying his sister's present and got into my car. As I drove, he gave me instructions on how to get there and I couldn't help but notice that he was getting more nervous the closer we got. As I pulled into her driveway, he had the look of a small child about to go into the dentist office.

Her house was an older, wood frame construction with old wood siding and a large covered front porch. Centered in the front on the porch was about a four foot high set of concrete steps. Several hanging plants that had withered in the winter air adorned the eve of the porch ceiling. An old porch swing swayed gently in the breeze creating a rhythmic creaking noise as the rusted chains rubbed against the metal hooks suspending it.

I helped Jim maneuver the steps and walk up to the door. There was no doorbell so I knocked gently on the wood screen door.

The main door opened and there stood a big bearded man looking through the screen. He was a big guy weighing about 280 pounds, wearing jeans, a camouflage shirt and big work boots. He just stood there for several seconds staring at Jim as though someone had ruined his whole day. Then he turned his eyes toward me as if he had just figured out who did it. Without a greeting or even a word of any kind, he turned back into the house and a few very awkward seconds later, Jim's sister appeared.

She stopped at the screen door and stared out for a few seconds and I begin to think that we were going to get the same treatment from her. Then she opened the screen door and put her arms around Jim and asked us to come inside.

The living room was cluttered with wrapping paper and a small artificial tree flashed away in one corner. The walls had pictures of kids and one of their wedding day, which appeared to be a courthouse in the background.

Of course there were decorations provided by her husband as well. I was guessing the room was only about 12 feet by 12 feet which seemed a little small for eight deer heads. But that was just my opinion. I was not a decorator or a hunter.

After giving her the present, which turned out to be a gift set full of different kinds of nuts in designer jars, she graciously invited us into the kitchen and sat us at the table and offered something to drink.

As her redneck husband sat in the living room watching television with the volume unusually high, Jim's sister sat and talked with us like a real lady genuinely concerned about Jim's welfare.

She, like Jim, looked to be older than she probably was. Her hair was evenly divided between black and gray and she had it up in the back like is common for women in this area. She had tired eyes but they looked right at you and not beyond or beside you. The lines in her face and the toughness of her hands and arms told me that she probably worked in a hosiery mill.

"You can come stay here," she pleaded. "You know that, don't you?"

"When he learns to pay some rent," bellowed the redneck as he came into the kitchen to get another beer.

"My brother does not have to pay rent in my home," she fired back.

"Oh hell, Thelma, we've had this talk a hundred times. He gets all that money from the government and what the hell does he do with it? Huh? He just blows it or something. If he stays here he's got to pay rent. That's all there is to it."

Upon that last commandment from the great redneck god, he grabbed his beer and returned to the living room.

"Don't worry about me, Sis," Jim said upon seeing the hurt in his sister's eyes. "Everything will be okay in a few months. You'll see."

A few months? Was he referring, I wonder, to the mysterious May 28th date he had mentioned earlier? As he sat there comforting his sister, I began to ponder what could possibly be going to happen on this date. It didn't make sense. I was worried at first that maybe he was planning on killing himself but who plans that out five months in advance.

Oh well, I knew that he would tell me if he wanted me

to know.

Finally convincing his sister that he was going to be all right, they gave each other a final hug and we said goodbye.

Driving back to Jim's car, there seemed to be a strange sense of satisfaction over us. Maybe it was because the visit seemed to go well. It was like we had charged the enemy's camp and came out victorious.

We pulled up alongside his car and I asked him to give me his keys so I could start his car and turn on the heater. As we sat there in my car allowing his to get warm, I took this opportunity to ask about Tommy, the guy who had saved his life in Vietnam.

"He was a character," Jim replied.

That's all he said. He just sat there smiling as if he was content that he had provided me with all the information there was on the subject.

"That's quite a story." My comment was so heavy with sarcasm that you could sense it dripping off the words. "You should go on Phil Donahue with that story."

"Okay," he admitted. "There's a little more to the story but I just don't feel like talking about it right now."

I could tell by his tone that he really didn't feel like talking about it right now so I dropped the subject. "Your car is still cranking good I see."

"Yes it is," he said in a better tone. "You did a hell of a job."

We sat there a few more minutes talking about meaningless stuff until we decided that his car was warm enough and that we didn't want the Sheriff's department looking for me.

"Goodbye," Jim said as he got out. "Thanks for going with me."

"Sure thing," I replied. "I'll see you around."

"Do you know the difference between work and home?" Skip's arms were waving in all directions as he walked circles around me yelling at the top of his lungs.

"Do you know the difference," he continued, "in a personal phone and a work phone?"

This was my first confrontation with Skip about staying on the phone but I could tell by his rhythm that these were rhetorical questions and I wasn't about to interrupt him with an answer.

"Are you going to answer me?" he screamed as he stopped to stare me directly in the eyes.

His face got just as red when he was mad as it did when he was laughing.

"It'll never happen again, boss," I blurted out. This was the only thing I could think to say considering I couldn't remember all the questions he had presented in his thirty-minute motivational seminar.

"Then get back to work," he added as a last inspirational note, "while you still have a job."

As I walked back up toward the pump islands, I could see Steven grinning from ear to ear. I knew that Steven would have fun with this all night. That was okay because I knew he, too, had stood there a time or two.

As our shift progressed we were glad to see night approach and bring some cooler air. It was only the first week in May but already it was getting hot. The canopy over the pumps kept the sun out but it seemed to keep the heat trapped under it.

It was Sunday night and business was slow as usual. I pulled out my History of Western Civilization book and started reading.

Steven gave me that 'what a dope' look but with finals less than two weeks away, I think he was wishing he had thought to bring some books, too.

About ten minutes from closing time, a motorcycle pulled up to the self-service pumps to get gas. I was still reading when I heard the rider walk up to Steven and say, "Seventy-five cents."

That sounded familiar.

As I watched him walk back to his bike, I suddenly realized that I hadn't seen Jim in a while. I had been so busy with school and finals and planning how to spend my Spring break that I hadn't even noticed that he had not been stopping by all the time. I couldn't even remember when the last day was that I had seen him.

"Steven, have you seen Jim lately?"

His eyebrows frowned as he stared upward at the light in the ceiling of the little booth. "Now that you mention it," he said, almost puzzled, "I haven't seen him in quite a few days. You don't think anything has happened to him, do you?"

"I don't know," I said as my mind started imagining different scenarios. "I hope not."

As I delved back into the Mesopotamian Empire, I tried to focus on events from 3800 years ago but I wasn't successful in that attempt. The formation of Babylon just didn't have any appeal at the moment. About as far back as I could get my mind to go was the Vietnam War and wondering what had happened to Jim over there. And more importantly, what's happened to him lately?

I suddenly felt like my mom and even pondered calling the Sheriff's office to see if they had any information. The more I thought about it, however, the more I couldn't bring myself to do it just for the fact that I was afraid that they may actually have information.

Later that evening, I saw a police car pull in to the self service pumps to get gas. I noticed Lane Preston getting out of the car so I walked over to say hello.

"Hey, Leo. How are you doing?"

"Can't complain, I guess."

"And if you did, who would listen? Right?" he replied.

I smiled and nodded. "Hey. Me and Steven there were just talking about Jim. We haven't seen him in several days now and I was wondering if you have."

He looked a little puzzled. "Now that you mention it, I haven't seen him either. I'll look in town tonight and see if I see him."

We talked for a little while longer and then he got into his squad car and drove away.

I walked back to the little booth and Steven was smiling.

"What?" I asked.

"He didn't pay for the gas."

We both laughed.

Actually, the city had an account and all the officers had to do was sign a ticket but without that signature, we didn't get paid.

Steven jokingly picked up the phone saying he was calling the police. I followed by saying that we might actually have to do that if he doesn't realize it himself and come back to sign.

I closed up my books and took them out to my car. It was useless trying to study. I tried to just concentrate on other things.

"So, Steven, how many girls are after you?"

I knew this would do the trick as Steven started rattling off names. He loved to talk about girls wanting him and I knew he wouldn't balk at the chance. What made it so funny was this conversation was very serious to him and he never realized that other guys got him to talk about it because it amused them.

Occasionally cars would pull up and interrupt his story but he always picked it right back up where he had left off.

I started to become aware of the fact that Officer Preston wasn't coming back and it was nearing closing time. Another ten minutes and I was contemplating calling the police department when Officer Preston came pulling back to the car wash.

He told me that he had been through town several times but could not locate Jim's car anywhere. He added that he would go by his sister's house the next day and ask her.

I told him about the ticket and he seemed a little embarrassed but signed the slip of paper and handed it back to me. "You should have called the police," he smiled.

As he drove away I began to worry more about Jim. Getting off work that night I decided to drive through town and have a look for myself.

Steven took the deposit to the bank as I went in the other direction.

There were a few places that he always liked to park because the business owners didn't give him a hard time. I searched one after another but had no luck. Finally, I headed home.

The next day I went to work at two o'clock like normal. Everything was the same. The night passed without a sign of Jim. To make matters worse, Officer Preston, likewise, did not pay a visit all night so we were left completely in the dark.

Steven had said something to Skip and he called me into the office later that afternoon. "No ideas about Jim?"

"None."

"What about his sister? Do you think he may be there?" Skip asked.

"I can't imagine that," I said. "And even if he was there, he would still come by here. The cop friend of Jim's is supposed to go by there today and check, though."

Skip nodded and I turned to go back to work.

The night passed slowly with no word until we were leaving to go home. As I was about to pull onto Main Street, a car came driving into the car wash with an arm waving out of the window.

My initial thought was that it was someone needing gas, but as the car pulled up alongside me, I noticed that it was Jim's sister.

"Ms. Thelma," I said, realizing that I didn't even know her last name.

"I was hoping I would catch you before you left," she said.

"Is everything all right? I mean, we were just talking about how we haven't seen Jim in a while. Do you know where he is?"

"He's at my house," she said nodding her head. "His car finally quit on him and now he's acting as if a loved one has died. I really think there's something wrong with his relationship with that car.

I'm really worried about how he's been acting and I was hoping maybe you could go by and see him. Maybe that would cheer him up."

"Sure," I offered. "I'm off tomorrow night so I'll come by after classes."

As I drove home that night, I began to worry also as I remembered the mysterious May 28th date that was now just a few weeks away.

The following day at school was no better with classes seeming to drag on as my thoughts lay elsewhere. Finally, however, my last class was over and I was heading back to town.

As I arrived at the house, I realized that it was only 1:30 in the afternoon and neither Thelma nor the redneck was yet home from work.

I knocked on the door a couple of times but never heard any movement. Finally I opened the door and called Jim's name followed by, "It's me, Leo."

I was debating on whether or not to take a chance and go on in when I heard Jim's cane tapping on the hardwood floor. He came into view grinning and waving me on in like I was sneaking in something illegal.

I followed him into the back bedroom. He sat down in a recliner and motioned for me to have a seat on the bed. The room was pretty dark, the only light coming from a small black and white television sitting on top of the dresser. The sound was all the way down. Looking back at Jim I noticed he was still grinning, a far better image than the ones I had imagined I would find.

"I was hoping you would come by," he said, finally breaking the silence. "Your station still able to produce a profit without my business?"

We both laughed at the idea of his seventy-five cents a

day, or lack thereof, making a difference. I was beginning to feel better already. Had his sister exaggerated his demeanor I wondered, or was he in fact this glad to see me?

"I heard your car quit on you."

"Yep," he replied. "Turns out he was in worse shape than I am."

"What happened?" I asked.

"Cruising down the road and 'BAM', threw a rod right through the motor. I didn't know what had happened at first. I just heard a loud noise and it started smoking.

"Okay," he added, noticing the smile on my face, "it started smoking more than normal.

"I had it towed to Gentry's Auto Shop and they told me it would need a new motor. They also said it could use a new transmission, a new radiator, new shocks, new brakes, and a new set of tires wouldn't hurt. They did mention that the alternator appeared to be in good shape.

So I junked it. It was going to cost me an arm and a leg to get fixed and that's more than I have on me."

I couldn't help but laugh. It amazed me how he could make fun of his situation.

"I figured I could handle staying here for a short time," he concluded.

"That's right," I said. "That special day is just around the corner. May the 28th I believe it was."

"You have a good memory," he said smiling.

That wasn't true at all. I'm the most absent-minded person I know. I usually can't remember names, dates, or numbers at all but this date stuck in my memory like glue.

"So," I continued before he could change the subject, "wanna tell me what's so special about that day?"

"Sure I do," he said, "right after lunch. I'm hungry. Are you hungry?"

I shook my head as he pushed himself up out of the chair and walked into the kitchen. I just sat there and watched as he made a ham and cheese sandwich, grabbed a soda from the fridge, and sat down to eat, occasionally looking up with a smirk on his face as if he had a winning lottery ticket in his pocket.

As he finished, I heard the front door open. Fearing that it might be the all too friendly redneck, I was relieved to see his sister walk into the kitchen. She came and sat at the table with us and told me how glad she was that I stopped by. She kept smiling at Jim as if she was surprised to see him in such a good mood.

I guess he really had been down in the dumps after his car died.

We sat there and talked and joked for an hour. It was great. Even though I enjoyed watching Jim and his sister enjoy talking with each other, I felt just a little sorry that she had possibly interrupted Jim's promise to explain the 28th of May.

I heard the front door open again and my hopes sank knowing that with his sister already here, that narrowed the choices on which family member this might be.

The redneck walked into the kitchen looking at Jim as if he had just wrecked his brand new car. He looked to be wearing the same camouflage shirt, jeans, and work boots.

Jim just kept smiling and asked, "Hey, Robert, how was your day today?"

Without saying a word, he went straight to the fridge, took out a beer, stood there a moment and stared at me as if I'm the one that had given Jim the keys to his new car, then walked into the living room and turned on the television.

We all laughed.

"Leo," Thelma asked after regaining her composure,

"would you like something to eat or drink?"

"I'm fine. Thank you," I replied

"We got business to complete anyway," Jim said as he got to his feet.

Walking back into the bedroom and assuming our original seats I asked, "Does this mean that you're going to tell me now?"

"I'm going to tell you everything," he said. "A deal's a deal."

"What does that mean?" I asked.

"This is your payment for putting the alternator on my car. Remember? I tried to pay you that night but you wouldn't take any money. You said if I would tell you the story behind the Purple Heart, then we'd be even. Well, today we break even."

"I graduated from high school in 1968."

Jim was looking toward me when he began telling the story but I noticed his eyes were not focused on me but somewhere beyond me in the distance. The more he talked, the farther away his vision drifted.

"I remember getting several graduation cards from aunts and uncles but it was one particular card I received from Uncle Sam that stands out most of all.

"I had heard what was going on over in Vietnam but never thought that I would be invited. It's not that I had any concrete plans on what I was going to do with my life after school, but it would have been nice to at least have had a choice.

"There were four of us from that class shipped off at the same time. We were sent to Fort Brag over in Georgia for basic training.

"After basic training, I got set up with the 101st Airborne which was pretty cool because I actually liked jumping out of planes.

"Of course, later I was sent to Nam. My unit was sent to a remote sandy beach area along some river in Vietnam. I never even knew what the name of the river was. Things were pretty good here. We took marches every other day, loaded and unloaded supplies, but mostly we would have cook outs, football games, or whatever we felt like doing.

"I couldn't figure out why I had been through all that training just to move cargo around but I wasn't complaining.

"It was during this time that I met three guys that would from that point be called my best friends.

"There was Willie Richards from Evansville, Texas. He was a tall lanky kid with small rim glasses. We called him Cowboy even though he admitted he had never even been on a horse.

"Mitchell Bengal from Highpoint, North Carolina was a weight lifter. He was about 5'8" tall and could run over you like a freight train. We called him Tiger for obvious reasons.

"They called me Bino in case you were wondering because of my light blonde hair was almost white.

"Then there was Doc. Tommy MacReynolds came from a small town in Wyoming called Oakview. He described it as a small mill town with less than a thousand in population.

"He was short and small. He had never played any sports but was the smartest man I've ever met.

"Tiger, Cowboy, and myself were all about the same age, fresh out of high school with a love for any full contact sport we could get into.

"Usually, while we were playing football, Doc was sitting over on the sideline reading a book, usually a medical journal of some kind. Doc was several years older and on the surface you may wonder what drew the other three of us to him. But there was something about Doc. He was like the wise older brother that was always quietly looking out for you. He was in his 3rd year of college when he got drafted. He said his plans were to go on to medical school and become a doctor but he already knew more about medicine than anyone I'd ever known. That's why we called him Doc.

"Growing up in a poor family meant he had to work two jobs while paying his way through school. You had to know him, though. He was the type of person that really appreciated the fact that he could work this hard to achieve what he wanted instead of complaining about it.

"To compound financial matters, his girlfriend had gotten pregnant right out of high school and they had gotten married shortly thereafter. His little daughter, Mandy, was four years old at this point and as much as he talked about her and showed off pictures we all felt like we were her father.

"I never understood why he was drafted. I had thought that being in college or having a small child would keep you off the list but I guess I was wrong. He never said anything about it so I didn't give it any more thought.

"We asked him once if he planned to go back and finish college when he got home and he just shook his head, pulled out Mandy's picture and said that she was all that mattered now.

"He said, 'She's going to be the doctor in this family. I don't care what I have to do, I'm going to send her through medical school and she's going to make me so proud.'

"Doc was like that. He was the most selfless person I have ever met. If he were starving he would share his food with you. If he were freezing he would give you his coat. Every person in the platoon came to Doc for advice on whatever was bothering them, be it problems at home or here, and It didn't matter if he had any useful advice for them or not, they always felt better just for talking with him.

"I remember one day, after we had been there for about six months, Doc was sitting out by the river looking sort of sad. This was uncharacteristic of him so I sat down beside him and ask what was wrong.

"'I was just reading this letter from my wife. She sent

me this picture of Mandy from Easter.'

"He handed me the picture and said, 'I just miss them, that's all.'

"As I sat there looking at Mandy in her little Easter dress, I heard the distant sound of a motor coming from down river. We usually got a supply boat about twice a week but this was not the chugging sound that I was familiar with.

"We called for the Sergeant. Sergeant Clay came to the bank and looked down the river with his binoculars.

"'That's our replacements,' he yelled. 'Everyone get your stuff together.'

"Our replacements? I couldn't believe it. I was told that a tour consisted of at least nine months to a year but we had only been over here for about seven. I wasn't complaining, however, and I rushed to my tent to pack my gear.

"Looking back now I can't believe how gullible I was in thinking that we were going home.

"A boat ride and a flight aboard a C-31 transport later and we soon found ourselves under a large canopy tent sitting on fold out chairs listening to a Colonel give us instructions on our mission.

"That confirmed that we were not going home.

"We were at a small camp only about fifty miles from the North Vietnamese border. Our orders were to take a hill called Dong Ap Bia from the Vietcong.

"I don't know why we needed that hill. It didn't seem to me to offer any kind of significance.

"Although we had been at a supply base for the last six months, we all had heard the stories of what was going on in this area. Now we were about to find out first hand. There wasn't one of us that wasn't scared.

"In one week we went from throwing footballs to throwing hand grenades. Even though we had trained for combat in basic training, it did not come close to the real thing. For days I never even saw what we were shooting at. The trees and bushes on the hill were so thick that most of the time, if I saw anything at all, it was flashes of gunfire followed by the sound of the bullets tearing up the ground all around us.

"The fighting went on for about three straight days until one morning it was like someone had called a temporary truce. We pulled back about a mile and set up camp.

"To this day I don't know what happened. I'm not sure who won that battle. I begin to think that the opposing commanding officers met and decided we were wasting too much ammunition and decided to take a day to rest. Whatever the reason, it felt like getting a weekend pass from pounding rocks all week,

"It gave me, Tiger, Cowboy, and Doc time to sit down and collect our thoughts. We were sitting around the tent that second night and Doc seemed to be in a real strange mood.

"He reached into his pocket and pulled out three pieces of paper and handed one to each of us. Each one had a drawing of Mandy. We always complained because he wouldn't give us any of the pictures he got of her so he had taken the time to draw us each a picture. They were beautiful, too. Each was very detailed, looking just like the picture he had used to go by.

"We never even knew he was an artist.

"'You want to know what I'm most afraid of?' he asked.

"'Getting an AK-47 shoved up your ass?' Tiger blurted out.

"We all got a good laugh out of that, even Doc. When the laughter subsided and the silence crept back upon us, Doc continued.

"'My greatest fear is that I won't be able to take care

of my daughter the way that I want to. What if I'm not able to send her to medical school for some reason? What if, for some reason, none of the dreams I have for her come true?'

"'That can't happen,' said Cowboy. 'Hell, the girl has got four dads. If we find out that you're messing up, we'll come up there and kick your ass.'

"Doc finally started smiling again. Then he stuck out his hand palm down and said, 'Okay, that settles it. You guys are now honorary godfathers.'

"We all put our hands on top of his and gave them one good shake to seal the deal.

"The next morning we were back in action. Apparently our leaders had decided that we had to take this hill. Trenches were already dug along the base on the east side and we took cover there. The C.O. decided we needed some lookout points along the west side of the hill about two hundred yards away. Several three-man teams were sent.

"Me and Tiger and Cowboy made up one of the lucky teams.

"We hurried across the ground and took cover behind a small bunker and quickly dug a fox hole for better cover. The other teams were about sixty yards away parallel to us on both sides. We each took a different direction and searched the top of the hill looking for the enemy.

"'Cowboy,' I whispered, 'if you were an Indian, what would your name be right now at this moment?'

"'Sitting Duck,' he answered.

"Exactly what I was thinking.

"I told Cowboy to keep his eyes open as I sank back into the foxhole and sat with my backpack up against the wall.

"It was humid as Hell. It felt like Bama in mid-summer.

"Actually, with all that equipment on, it made me think of spring training in football.

"I played on our high school team.

"You played football, didn't you? What position did you play?"

Huh? I'm sorry. Did we go to commercial? My mind was trying to catch up with the fact that he just interrupted his own story at the climax.

"What did you say? What's the matter with you? You can't change the subject. Finish the story."

"Just wanted to make sure you were paying attention," he laughed

"I was just relaxing," he continued, "thinking about better times when suddenly all hell broke loose. We could hear gunfire coming from the direction of where we just left. It sent shivers up and down my spine. Part of me was glad not to be there and part of me was feeling guilty.

"Cowboy, Tiger and me were all up and ready. We started scanning the ridge looking for any signs of movement.

"Suddenly we could hear shouting from several different people. It was faint at first and overlapping so we couldn't make out what they were saying. Then we clearly heard the Sergeant's voice yelling for us to get the hell out of there.

"Then everything went completely white. I remember my ears burning but I couldn't hear anything. As I rolled over onto my stomach, the first thing I became aware of was that I was no longer in the hole. I was actually several feet from it. I'm not sure if I got there on my own power or not.

"As my eyes began to focus again, I could see one of the other lookout teams running back toward the trenches. As my eyes followed them, I noticed soldiers only about thirty yards away lying on their stomachs firing directly over our heads up the hill.

"Picking up movement beside me, I turned to see Cowboy and Tiger rolling around in pain.

"The soldiers firing on the ground behind us were soon completely covered by smoke, some from mortar blasts and some from their own gunfire.

"Then I saw a sight that I will never forget. Doc appeared, running through the smoke directly toward us. I recall thinking that for a man who never played football with us, he would have made a hell of a wide receiver.

"As he got about twenty feet from us, I saw the impact in his right shoulder and the blood burst outward. The force of the shot knocked his upper body backwards but he was running so fast that his feet continued forward much like a ball player sliding into home.

"Angry now, I started looking around for my rifle. Then I felt someone grab me and lift me up. It was Doc. He threw me over his shoulder and then positioned himself between Cowboy and Tiger, squatted down and grabbed both of them by the backpack straps, stood up and started running.

"You would have to see Doc to know what an amazing feat this was. He really looked like your classic nerd from high school that you might find on the chess team with the pocket protector in his shirt pocket.

"There he ran, though, carrying and dragging the three of us.

"The smoke was starting to drift farther across the field, which was providing us with some cover. I was hanging over his left shoulder and could see that Cowboy and Tiger were both unconscious at this point.

"Then a bullet ripped into Doc's hamstring and he went down again. As soon as he hit the ground, he got back up again. I could see the blood was all the way down his pants leg already.

"I pulled my hamstring once during a football game and couldn't play for four weeks. I didn't know how he was doing it.

"Finally I saw the field medics grabbing for us and then I blacked out. I awoke in a helicopter. I thought at first I was dreaming because Lane was there, a guy I had went through high school and basic training with. I remember him telling me that Tommy was dead.

"The next time I was conscious, I was in a M.A.S.H. unit and both my legs from the knees down were gone. I then found out that Tiger had lost complete sight in one eye and fifty percent in the other.

"Cowboy took the blunt of the blast with third degree burns over most of his body. Before it would be over, he would end up losing several fingers and have a steel plate put in his head.

"The physical pain we were feeling, however, was nothing compared to learning that Doc was indeed dead. Turned out he had gotten shot a total of nine times getting us to safety. Although none of them struck any vital organs, he still bled to death before the medics could get there.

"We three received a Purple Heart and were sent home. Tommy received the Silver Star and it was awarded to his family."

The story was over. Jim sat back in the recliner and stared at the far wall. I sat there in silence also as I soaked in the whole thing.

Finally Jim looked at me and asked, "We're even now?"

I nodded.

"Good," he said, "because I'm ready to go into debt again."

"What does that mean?" I asked wearily.

"I can't tell you right now."

"Well, there's a surprise," I shot back.

"I know you have finals coming up. You just con-centrate on that and when your tests are over, come see me again."

As I drove home that evening, it suddenly dawned on me that he never did tell me what May 28th was about.

Finals were split up into three different days at Northeast State. All of mine fell on the first two days.

As I drove to school that first morning, I had a panic attack wondering if I had studied enough. Once I started taking my first test, which was Trigonometry, my fears were laid to rest as I easily cruised through the exam. Western Civ followed and was equally effortless.

The first two were over with only Computer Programming to go the next day. That class was a breeze, however, and I had little concern about it. The worst part was behind me.

Driving home from school that day, I was confident that I should finish my first year with at least a 3.8 GPA.

Driving out the dirt road heading home that afternoon, I noticed several cars, including a police car at Granny's house. I shook my head wondering what she had done now.

I pulled off the road in front of her house and walked up to see what was going on.

"Hey," Mom said as she noticed my car and walked out of Granny's house.

"What's up?" I asked. I couldn't help but notice that Mom was trying not to laugh.

She held up her index finger as if to tell me to wait and

she would fill me in.

The police officer then came out of the house and I noticed he, too, was smiling. He got in his car and drove away.

The only one not smiling was Granny as she walked out on the porch cussing under her breath.

Mom then filled me in on the whole story.

A bull in the pasture across the street from Granny's had been jumping the fence and getting into her garden. She apparently had already run the bull away several times trying to let him know that the buffet was closed. This day she had decided a firmer warning was in order. She took her double barrel shotgun and, according to her, fired into the air and scared the bull back into the pasture.

This was almost accurate.

While she had fired into the air, she failed to mention that she had fired into the air which occupied the space directly between her and the bull. The bull did jump back into the pasture but with a load of buckshot in his hind quarters.

The officer was doing a report and luckily the owner of the bull wasn't interested in pressing charges. Granny still didn't understand that what she had done was wrong since it was on her property.

I'm sad to say that the bull had to be put down.

The next day I drove to school to take my last final.

Mr. Gains, the computer instructor, came in to administer the exam. It actually consisted of problems on paper that had to be completed on the computer.

Although the problems were quite simple, the little green numbers and letters on the black screen kept drifting out of focus as my mind wondered. I finally convinced myself that if I didn't stop worrying about other things, I would never get out of there.

I buckled down and finished the test ahead of everyone

else. I printed the computer section and turned it in with the handout and left.

I got into my car and hurried to town.

I stopped by a fast food joint for a quick lunch and then on to see Jim to find out what the crazy old coot had up his sleeve now.

Knowing him was like watching those old time cliff-hangers on television. They'd have you right on the edge of your seat and then make you wait until the next week to find out what happened.

I parked on the curb to leave the driveway clear for Thelma and the redneck.

Waving me on into his sister's house much like before, I followed him into the kitchen where he had been playing solitaire on the table. He sat down, and without so much as a word, resumed the game he had already started.

I didn't say a word, but rather just waited until the game played out. If I had learned anything about Jim, it was that he would talk about something when he was ready and not one minute before.

He stacked the cards up in a neat stack, looked at me and said, "May 28th."

Leaning my head slightly forward, I raised my eye-brows to let him know that he had my attention and to continue.

"Mandy graduates from high school."

"Mandy?" I asked. "Doc's Mandy? Is that who you're talking about? Mandy MacReynolds?"

"The one and only," he smiled.

"So what does that mean?" I asked. "How does that affect you?"

"I never did finish the story," he began.

"After Doc was killed, the three of us were transferred

from the M.A.S.H. unit to a rehabilitation facility were we spent a couple of months before coming stateside. We talked about Doc and Mandy a lot.

"All of Doc's belongings were sent home but we each still had the drawing of Mandy that he had given to us. We remembered that last night how he was worried that he wouldn't be able to take care of her and how he made us all honorary godfathers.

"It was at that point that we made a pact between us that we've all kept to this day. We decided that we would save as much of our disability pay as we could, or any other source of income we might make, using only enough to exist on, and putting the rest into a trust fund for Mandy's education.

"Over the last 14 years we've managed to average about $700 a month between us. With the interest the account has accumulated, the balance now stands at $143,244 and some change. We plan to present her with this check when she graduates from Oakview High School on May 28th. Then she can go to medical school if she wants to without any problems."

"How do you know she's still there and that she is for sure graduating?" I asked.

"Because we've been keeping tabs on her. Tiger and his wife live in Idaho Falls, which is only about two hours from there. Every few months or so we contact him for a status report.

"Our plan was simple. One of us wearing our army uniform would approach her after the graduation ceremony and tell her we were with the records department. Then we'd explain how her father started an educational trust fund for her when he was in the service that would mature upon her graduation and then present her with the check.

"Two things I didn't foresee, however, was that my car would quit on me just before her graduation and also that none of us can actually pass for active soldiers now.

"We really need someone in better shape.... younger."

Several seconds of silence passed.

"With transportation."

Several more seconds passed.

"Whoa! Wait a minute!" I yelled as what he was implying was starting to sink in.

"You said you wanted to go somewhere for Spring Break," he said grinning. "Here's your chance."

"Yeah," I argued, "but I was thinking more along the lines of Florida, you know, the beach, bikinis..."

We argued back and forth a while, me with a grimace on my face, him with a grin. Finally I started giving it some thought.

It wasn't that he was making any good points by any stretch of the imagination; it was just that the prospect of meeting the people in the story had quite an appeal to me.

I finally told him that I would have to talk it over with my parents and get back to him.

On the way home, however, I stopped by the car wash and talked to Skip.

After explaining the situation to him, I was surprised by his response. "Hell, can I come with you?"

"So you think I should go?" I asked.

"I'll say this," Skip said in a sincere voice that I'd never heard him use before, "If you don't go, you'll never forgive yourself."

That really boosted my confidence as I drove on home to tell Mom and Dad. It went pretty much as I expected. They were still arguing when I went to bed.

As I lay there in bed that night, I kept weighing the

pros and cons of this trip. Actually, all I could think of were pros. The only cons I could think of were mostly outrageous hypothetical cases like what if the world really is flat and we drive off the end of it.

I guess deep down my mind was made up.

The morning of the 25th, I was packed and ready to go. Dad gave me some money and told me to drive carefully. Mom hugged me and told me to call every time we stopped to get gas so she wouldn't have to keep checking in with every state trooper's office between here and Idaho.

Skip had given me the time off work with instructions to tell him the whole story upon returning.

I guess I was as ready as I could be. Now to stop by and pick up Jim and we would be on our way.

Jim was sitting on his sister's porch with a large duffel bag beside him. His sister came out to see us off while the redneck watched silently from the doorway.

I put his bag in the trunk, told her we would call when we got there, offered a final wave, and we were on our way.

Roughly 2300 miles lay before us. Our plan consisted of one of us driving at all times, stopping only for gas and food. This wasn't the most comfortable way to travel but with over 40 hours of driving time ahead of us, it was the only way to insure we got there in time.

At times Jim would tell more stories about Doc which would really help the time pass.

"We had only been at the supply base in Nam a couple of weeks. This was before any of us had gotten to know each other, before the nicknames.

"We were playing a game of football and Cowboy and I were on one team and Tiger was on the other. Tiger was running over us pretty bad. I remember every person on our team getting frustrated trying to figure a way to stop him.

"The next time in the huddle, Cowboy looks at me and says, 'We gotta stop this guy. You men on the line let him come through and then you hit him high and I'll hit him low.'

"That was dirty play. You could really injure someone that way. I was all for it.

"The next play they handed the ball to Tiger and he came right up the middle, right through the hole the guys had left for him. As soon as he had gotten past the linemen, Cowboy and I merged on him with perfect timing. As Cowboy took his legs out from under him, I was doing my best to remove his head from his torso. It worked like a charm. Tiger did a 180 in mid air and landed directly on the top of his head, rolled over a couple of times and came to rest on his back completely unconscious.

"At first I was afraid that we had killed him. But let me tell you something; that son-of-a-bitch never dropped the ball.

"Suddenly Doc appeared and knelt down beside him. He told someone to go get some water and a cloth. Tiger's eyes opened when Doc started running water over his head and he then instructed two guys to get him to his feet and start him walking.

"'You'll be fine,' Doc said, 'just a slight concussion.'.

"Tiger said, 'I just need to lie down for a while.'

"'Oh no. You can't lie down,' Doc argued. 'If you have a concussion and fall asleep you might not wake up.'

"Suddenly Cowboy yells, 'Oh shit! Look at my finger.'

"In the excitement of Tiger being knocked cold, Cowboy hadn't even noticed his own injury. He was standing there holding his hand out in front of him and his little finger was literally forming the letter T.

"'My finger's broke,' he yelled.

"'It's not broken,' Doc replied, 'it's just popped out of

joint. Here, let me see it.'

"Doc took Cowboy's arm under his own arm, positioned his grip on the dislocated finger, and quickly popped in back in place. Cowboy held up his hand to reveal the finger was indeed back to normal. "'I can't hardly bend it,' he says.

"'It will be swollen for a few days,' Doc said. 'Just try to be careful with it. It will leave a knot on your joint though.'

"'For how long?' he asked.

"'Until you die,' Doc says.

"Turns out that Doc was actually wrong about that one. Ironically, that turned out to be one of the fingers Cowboy lost after the incident.

"Anyway, we were all impressed with his knowledge of injuries.

"'What are you?' I asked, 'some kind of doctor?'

"'Sort of,' he replied, 'but I think you guys are playing too rough. Maybe you should tone it down a little.'

"'Hell, he ain't a doctor,' Tiger shouted. 'He's my mother.'

"Several of the guys started laughing and ragging Doc pretty hard about then. Doc just smiled.

"Then someone yelled, 'What kind of doctor are you, a gynecologist?'

"'Well I sure feel like one today,' Doc said as he stared around at everybody, 'caused I've never seen so many pussies in my life.'

"There was about five seconds of silence as Doc's insult sank home.

"You had to see Doc standing there among all these guys, most of them pretty good size lads, who were just playing full tackle football with no protective gear at all and here was Doc looking like a reject from the chess club. There wasn't one guy there who couldn't kick Doc's ass from here to sundown with one arm tied behind their back.

"I guess it was this very thought that made this moment so funny. Whatever it was, everybody started laughing so hard that we had tears running down our cheeks. Some of the guys were literally rolling on the ground. It felt good to laugh like that considering where we were. It was nice to forget about what was going on around you even for just a brief moment.

"I think that was the beginning. That's when most people started liking Doc."

Throughout the night and next morning, I listened to more stories as we continued onward stopping only to get gas and eat.

Oh yeah, and to call my mom.

❧10❧

It was a little after 6:00 in the morning on May 27th when we pulled into the driveway of Mitchell 'Tiger' Bengal in Idaho Falls, Idaho.

It was in an older neighborhood but what appeared to be a pretty good area of town. The homes were fairly small but neat with neatly kept lawns and a mix of moderately priced automobiles.

There were two other vehicles in his driveway: a fairly new black Chevy Van which had an Idaho tag so I assumed it to belong to them, and an older model faded red Ford Pickup sporting a camper shell with a Texas tag.

The house was brick and had a privacy fence encasing the back yard as did several other houses on the block. I could see the top of a small RV peaking out over the fence along one side of the house.

I was glad that the drive was over but my first thought was that we had gotten here too early in the morning. The grass was still wet with dew. A small rolled up newspaper with a rubber band around it lay close to the small set of concrete steps on the front of the small covered porch.

"Maybe we should go get breakfast and come back," I said, worrying that they were still asleep.

Jim just smiled and headed right on up to the door and

started knocking. A few seconds of silence passed and then it was if the whole house came to life as sounds of shuffling feet and muffled voices bridged the thickness of the front door.

The door opened and there stood Tiger, Tiger's wife, and Cowboy all standing in a line motioning us to come in. They were all smiling and looked so happy. They reminded me of kids on Christmas morning after having waited all year for this day.

I had prepared myself for feeling a little outside this group and maybe even being treated so, but that was not the case. Cowboy and Tiger both shook my hand, called me by name, and told me how glad they were that I had brought Jim. Tiger's wife hugged me and told me how glad she was to see me. It was incredible. I have visited family members and not received a welcome like this.

We all had a seat in the living room as we answered questions about the trip. Jim and I sat on the sofa and Cowboy and Tiger sat in two dining room chairs that they had carried into the living room.

Helen was still wearing her robe so she excused herself to go change.

"Find it alright?" Tiger asked me.

"Oh yeah. Good directions. Drove straight here," I replied.

Tiger turned and smiled at Cowboy.

"What?" Cowboy snapped. "So I got a little lost."

Jim and Tiger laughed. "The sad part is that he's been here a couple of times before." Tiger added.

"They've added several roads since then." Cowboy was determined to not let them get the last word.

"He's right," Helen said as she came back into the living room. She had on jeans and a sweat shirt now. "They have done a lot of road construction in the last year. I get lost myself sometimes."

Cowboy crossed his arms and smiled. He seemed glad that someone was taking his side.

It was amazing to me that I was really sitting here with these guys. I could tell who was who even though there had been no introductions. Tiger was still a fairly muscular figure with dark hair and a thick mustache. He was wearing glasses and I later noticed that one lens was just glass as was the eye behind it.

Cowboy was about 6 feet tall with a small frame but with a bit of a beer belly. He wasn't wearing glasses at all. I don't know if he wore contacts now or not. You could easily see the burn scars down one side of his face and on both arms. The fact that he was missing the last two fingers on his right hand and his index finger on his left was also a dead giveaway.

Tiger's wife, Helen, decided to start breakfast since everyone was here and awake.

I sat in the living room with the guys and listen to them catch up on the last 15 years. I learned that Tiger and Helen had a son who was eight years old and a daughter who was six and they were staying with friends so that we would have more room in the house during our stay.

Helen taught elementary school and Tiger was a warehouse supervisor at a local food distribution center.

I was surprised to find out that Tiger had never drawn disability at all.

Cowboy, who had arrived ahead of us by a day, appeared to have had a rougher go of things. He had been married twice but divorced from each with no children. He still lived in the town where he had grown up and had been through several odd jobs over the years to supplement his government check but had not stuck with anything. He was a genuinely easy-going person but I sensed there was still some bitterness over how his life had turned out.

When breakfast was ready, we sat at the dining room table and ate in relative silence. Just the occasional small talk about present day events was offered up as conversation.

Afterwards, after returning to the living room, the meal coupled with our long drive took its toll on me and as I sat back on the sofa I drifted off to sleep.

When I awoke, everyone in the room was staring at me grinning. I was embarrassed at first wondering if I had been snoring or something.

"What?" I asked.

"Just waiting on you to wake up," Jim answered.

"That's right," Tiger added. "We've got work to do."

I was still groggy and started to wonder what work he was referring to. If it had been my dad, I would have expected it to mean picking orca or something along those lines.

I got up and followed them outside and we all got into Tiger's van and headed into town. Although I was curious where we were going, I didn't say a word.

"You sure you can drive okay with one eye?" I asked before thinking.

"Hell," Tiger shot back, "I still got one more eye on the road than most drivers."

"He didn't always have that glass eye, you know," Cowboy said. "His first one was made of wood."

"Really?" I asked, actually believing every word of it.

"Yes sir," Cowboy went on. "And he was real self conscious about it. For a long time he wouldn't even leave the house. Finally I talked him into going to a dance at the VFW. He was too scared to ask anyone to dance cause he was afraid they would make fun of his eye.

"Then I saw this really big fat girl sitting by herself over by the wall and I told Tiger to go ask her to dance because there was no way she would turn him down."

At this point in the story, I was shaking my head at my own gullibility for even letting myself think that this was a true story.

Cowboy continued. "So Tiger gets up his nerve and walks up to this girl and asked if she would like to dance.

"She says, 'Would I.'

"Tiger got real mad and said, 'I may have a wood eye but you're a fat cow.'"

We all laughed except Tiger who just shook his head. "Do you have any idea how many times I've heard that lame joke?"

We were still laughing when we got to our destination. The sign above the entrance to the store read BIG AL'S ARMY SURPLUS.

I had forgotten about this part of the plan.

I began to get nervous and it was a whole day before the graduation. We went from rack to rack picking out the right size articles to compile my ensemble. We had put together a nice looking army uniform with the only glitch being that the shirt already had corporal stripes on the arms and a name patch that read 'Schmitt.'

From there it was a trip to the barber for a typical army haircut to complete the image. It was somewhat cool I suppose to have all this attention but deep down I was feeling rather gullible for letting them talk me into this.

As I sat there while the barber used an electric trimmer to cut my hair down to a quarter of an inch, I noticed everyone smiling.

It wasn't a big deal since I normally kept my hair very short anyway.

"What are you smiling at?" I looked at Jim. "You're

next."

Cowboy and Tiger joined in as they ribbed Jim about his long white strands.

After I was finished, I was surprised to see Jim get up and take a seat in the barber chair. He had the barber give him a nice cut. It wasn't near as short as mine but actually looked pretty good as the barber parted it on one side. Then he really shocked me as he asked for a shave.

Upon returning to Tiger's house, it began to get a little weird. As Tiger grilled out steaks, Cowboy and Jim laid out the script while Helen and I played the roles of Mandy and Army Guy. This was rather embarrassing but I went through with it until I had the act down word-for-word.

When the steaks were ready, we sat and ate a great meal and drank cold beer. Spirits were very high at the table that night. It was like these men had been on a long hard journey for many years and had just come to their destination. It was quite an atmosphere of happiness as they toasted Doc, toasted each other, toasted me, and everyone toasted Mandy.

Laughter filled the house as they told their favorite stories about Doc and each other. I heard the same story of Tiger getting tackled from two other points of view and although each story differed in detail, it was still funny each time.

It was the first time since we had gotten here that they actually talked about the past.

I was amazed at the bond that still existed between them after all this time. They were really only together for a very short time, relatively speaking, but I guess it's not the amount of time you spend together as much as it is what happens to you in that time.

We sat and talked at the table until it was time to go to bed. I let Jim and Cowboy sleep in the kid's bedrooms and I took the couch.

An hour later I was still wide awake as I tried to get tomorrow's events out of my head. I went into the kitchen and got a glass of milk and sat there at the table hoping to get sleepy.

Helen appeared and I first feared that the light had awaken her.

"I was just going to the bathroom," she said, "and I saw this light."

I smiled and nodded.

She sat down at the table across from me. "Can't sleep, huh?"

I shook my head.

"Don't worry, you'll do fine. Then finally it'll be over."

I began to wonder how she really felt about this whole thing with her husband saving all this money for another man's child.

"How long have you known about this?"

"Since Mitch and I started dating. I thought it was the most wonderful thing I had ever heard of anyone doing. I still think that.

"Of course there were times over the years that I thought maybe he was putting too much money into it but I never said a word. He's always taken care of his family as well. We both work and do pretty well. We own this house so our bills are not that great.

"I grew up in this house. Did I tell you that?"

I smiled and shook my head.

"Yes. When my mother and father retired, they built a new home out in the country and we bought this one from them at a really good deal. I enjoyed growing up here so I knew my kids would, too.

"The only regret I have is that Mitch and I never had a real honeymoon. He always told me that when the kids were grown, he would make it up to me. He would say, 'Idaho Falls today, Niagara Falls tomorrow.' One day we will make it.

"It's Jim and Willie that this has had to be hard on. Mitch always felt a little guilty that he came out of the ordeal a lot better than they did.

"We bought that RV outside so we could go visit them over the years because we knew they wouldn't be able to come up here and it always broke Mitch's heart to see them and how they were living.

"I think there were times when he wanted to tell them to stop and keep their money so they could have some better things in life but I don't believe they would have listened anyway.

"I believe this day, having this goal, has been what's kept them going over the years."

We sat there and talked a while longer until we decided it was time to try and get some sleep.

Getting up from the table, she turned to go back down the hallway, then stopped and turned back. "Goodnight, Corporal Schmitt."

11

"Leo. Leo. Wake up."

I awoke to see Helen standing over me shaking my shoulder. My neck was stiff from using the sofa arm as a pillow. In fact, my whole body felt like it had been run over. I sat up and stretched trying to rejuvenate my muscles. I could smell coffee and hear whispered conversation coming from the kitchen. I got up and went in and sat at the table.

"Good morning," Tiger said. "Sleep well?"

"Oh yeah, like a baby."

Judging from the smile on his face, I was guessing that he had picked up on the sarcasm.

"You can use the shower in our bedroom," he continued. "Your clothes are laid out on the bed."

It was already seven o'clock. Mandy's graduation was scheduled for eleven and it was still a two hour drive.

I showered, shaved, and started putting on the uniform. I felt strangely calm this morning as I again rehearsed the lines in my head. I stood there looking into the mirror as I imagined handing a perfect stranger more money than I had ever seen. I practiced my salute just in case I ran into any real military personnel.

I had learned more about Army conduct in the last day than I had ever known.

Walking into the kitchen in full Corporeal Schmitt attire brought on the expected whistles and jeers.

"You look great," Helen comforted.

"Just one more thing," Tiger said.

Walking into the back room, he returned with a cigar box which he sat on the table then opened the top. Inside were several medals and patches. He began to pin them on my shirt explaining what each one was as he went.

"This one is for marksmanship. It's expert level unlike what other people in the room received."

Jim and Cowboy chuckled.

Tiger continued until I had a neat row of different medals adorning my uniform just above my left shirt pocket.

"This one is for when you screw up and we have to hurt you," he said smiling and holding up his own Purple Heart.

I just shook my head. "How can I go wrong with this kind of confidence behind me?"

We all laughed. Spirits were high and everyone was dressed up and ready to go. Even Jim looked very neat in nice clothes sporting his new haircut and clean shaven.

Tiger drove the van so we could all sit comfortably without having to take two vehicles. As we rode, I got to see some of the countryside in the daylight for the first time. It was beautiful. We entered Wyoming and passed through the edge of the Grand Teton National Forest. The large evergreens were incredible as they made me think of some of my favorite places back home.

We arrived at Oakview and drove directly to the schoolhouse. In fact, the school was the only evidence I saw that there was actually a town there. We followed other cars where they were parking along the side of a little road running beside the football field.

We parked and walked in the direction of the other spectators. I noticed that they had a stage and portable bleachers set up on the front lawn of the small brick school building.

It reminded me a lot of the little school that I had attended.

I noticed that the weather was quite pleasant and I realized that I had never seen an outdoor graduation ceremony before. It's way too hot this time of year back home to even consider it.

Younger students were handing out programs of the ceremony. We each took one and sat down at the bottom of the bleachers so Jim wouldn't have to climb any steps.

There was an area of folding chairs reserved for the parents that were positioned between us and the stage. Behind the stage was another group of folding chairs for the graduating class that set facing us.

Looking at the program, I noticed that there were only thirty-eight students graduating today. I scanned the names to find Mandy. Amanda Lanette MacReynolds: Beta club, OHS club, Math club, Debate team, and softball. She seemed to be pretty active.

As the seats begin to fill, Jim reminded me that after the ceremony they were going to head on back to the car while I did my thing. They knew it would look suspicious if they hung around to watch.

I was to tell her about the account her father had set up, get her to sign for the check, and leave. Tiger had it planned out pretty well. I had a folder with all these official looking documents to give merit to the story. Even the bank from which the check was written was a federal military credit union.

The graduating students were announced and slowly began to fill the seats behind the stage.

I felt a little nervous at first because we were in a direct line of vision with each other. I realized then that she would have no reason to notice me. No one else had paid any attention to me so why would she.

I was glad to discover that I was the only one there representing, or misrepresenting I should say, military personnel.

I looked them over trying to determine which one was Mandy. I couldn't tell. They were not seated according to the program which had them listed in alphabetical order. I would just have to wait until they called her name.

The ceremony started with the Principal giving his speech about becoming adults and going out into the world, conquering tomorrow, blah....blah....blah. It sounded strangely like the speech our Principal had used at my graduation a year ago. I began to wonder if there was a graduation speech guidebook.

Next came the Valedictorian and Salutatorian speeches which contained similar sentiments coupled with the elements of sorrow to express how much everyone would be missed.

Finally they started passing out individual diplomas. One-by-one they walked across the stage in their dark blue robes, shook the Principal's hand as they took their certificate, then walked off the other side of the stage and returned to their seat.

"Amanda Lanette MacReynolds," the Principal's voice rang out as the hairs on the back of my neck stood up.

Mandy strolled across the stage. A golden sash around her neck signified her place among the top grades in her class. I could not make out any features from where I was sitting, but I could see she was only about 5'2" with long sandy-brown hair that was neatly braided as it appeared from her cap and extended halfway down her back. She took her diploma and returned to her seat.

Jim, Cowboy, Tiger and Helen were all applauding vigorously. Only a few students remained after Mandy so they decided to go on back to the car and wait on me.

As I watched them walk away, I took several deep breaths as I felt a moment of anxiety. I calmed down, however, and sat back and watched the ceremony conclude as the Principal presented them as the graduating class of 1984 and all caps went flying into the air.

I got up and made my way through the crowd. People were hugging and taking pictures as I maneuvered my way to where most of the students were still huddled together.

I finally saw Mandy. She was standing with several other students and they were all laughing and enjoying the moment. She was quite attractive. She had on little or no makeup but still presented a beautiful complexion topped off with amazing blue eyes.

As I got within a few feet of her, she suddenly turned and started to walk away.

"Miss MacReynolds?" I yelled to get her attention.

She turned around and waited as I walked up to her. Her friends likewise waited to see what was going on.

"Miss MacReynolds," I went on. "I'm Corporal Travis Schmitt with the United States Army. If I could please have just a moment of your time."

She smiled and said, "I have nothing against the Army but like I told the other recruiters, I'm just not interested in joining the military."

"I'm not a recruiter, ma'am. I'm with the records department."

"Hey, get lost!" one of her male classmates said in his best macho voice.

They turned and started to hurry off.

"Miss MacReynolds," I blurted out in desperation. "It's about your father."

She stopped dead in her tracks and stood there facing away from me for a few seconds before turning around and slowly walking back to me. Again her friends stayed right by her side.

"What's this all about?" her macho friend asked, taking charge once again.

I ignored him once but this time I could feel the blood heat up behind my cheeks. "Sir, this is official business and does not concern you. I'm going to ask you once to not interfere. Now if you will please excuse us."

"It's okay," Mandy said. "You guys go ahead and I'll catch up with you later."

As her friends reluctantly went on, she turned and asked, "What is this about?"

"Your father was William Thomas MacReynolds, killed in action in Vietnam?"

She nodded. I could see her eyes mist up a little.

I opened the folder and continued.

"In the beginning of the Vietnam conflict, the Government started a program for soldiers and their offspring. Your father had taken advantage of this program and started it immediately after being drafted into the Army. It was an educational trust fund that the soldiers could put money into and the Government would match their contribution. The account would be in the child's name and continue to accrue interest until it matured upon the child's graduation from high school. In your case, that's today.

"The check is made out to you and although the Government can't control the way you use it, I'm suppose to remind you that it is for your future education."

Pulling the envelope and forms from the folder, I continued, "I just need you to sign and date this form acknowledging that you received this check and we'll be finished."

Her hands were shaking as she took the pen. When I handed her the envelope, I noticed tears rolling down her face. "This isn't right," she whispered.

"I assure you it's correct, Ms. MacReynolds," I replied.

"But my dad wasn't drafted. He volunteered."

"Oh," I stammered. "I just assumed that. That was my error. Sorry." How could we make such a mistake? I don't think even Jim, Cowboy or Tiger knew this.

As she read over the documents, she continued to cry. Finally, after what seemed like an eternity to me, she signed the paperwork.

Feeling the moisture welling up in my own eyes, I thanked her and congratulated her and quickly turned and walked away.

It was over. I had done it. I walked past the bleachers and was about to disappear behind the corner of the school building when I heard someone yelling. I turned back to see Mandy running toward me with a man and a woman.

"Wait!" Mandy was yelling.

Although my instincts were to run, I stood fast. The three of them came up to me, each one with a bewildered look on their face. They had obviously seen the amount of the check.

"Corporal," Mandy started, "this is my mother and stepfather."

I don't know why I hadn't thought that her mom would have remarried after all this time.

"Nice to meet you," I said as I extended my hand to them both.

"We don't understand this," her mom said. "It doesn't make sense. Tom was only in the service for about a year.

How could he have put that much money into a trust fund?"

"Well, the Government put money in also and it has been earning interest for a long time," I offered as a lame excuse.

"Still, it would never have come to this amount," the stepfather replied.

He seemed like a decent fellow. He was a little less than six feet with a very slim, muscular body. His veins in his arms extended all the way through his hands and into his fingers. He certainly seemed to be a man who worked for a living.

"It's not that we're not appreciative," he continued. "We think it's a Godsend. Lord knows that me and her mother had no idea how we were ever going to pay her way through medical school."

"You're planning on going to medical school?" I asked, trying to hold back my smile for fear that it would give me away.

"That's been my plan my whole life," she confirmed.

I felt reassured as we stood there. A few seconds of silence passed as I realized they were still waiting for an explanation.

"Look," I began, "this is classified information and I'm not supposed to be telling you this..."

Telling them what? I was totally improvising this whole thing at this point.

"I did look over the entire file before they sent me on this assignment."

Assignment? Great! Now I sound like James Bond.

"All I can tell you is that multiple donations were made to the fund every month for a long time after your father was killed. All we can assume is that your father had some really good friends over there with whom he must have shared his dreams of your education and they took it upon themselves to help out. It's really not that uncommon. Several of these cases I've seen had more than one contributor. Maybe it was not having children of their own combined with the bond that these men in combat developed for each other that inspired these actions. I really don't know. All I can tell you is that this is the total, it's yours, and good luck in medical school."

Judging from the humble look in their eyes, I figured I had satisfied them with my explanation. I turned and walked away, quite impressed with my own fabrication capabilities. Everyone was waiting for me in the van.

The drive back to Tiger's was a fun trip as I recounted the events for them. It was an incredible feeling of accomplishment even though I played such a small role in this whole ordeal.

Getting back to Idaho Falls early that afternoon, I had assumed we would head on back to Alabama. I packed my bag as Helen cooked grilled cheese sandwiches for lunch.

As we sat there and ate, the guys went on about how proud they were of Mandy and how Doc would be proud as well.

After we ate, I mentioned to Jim that maybe we should think about getting started. I noticed everyone was looking at me in kind of an odd way.

Jim pulled out an envelope and handed it to me and said, "You drive carefully. We want you to take your time and get a hotel room at night to sleep."

"You're not going?" I asked.

Jim shook his head.

I opened the envelope to reveal $500 in cash.

"I don't deserve this."

"That's from all of us," Cowboy said. "It's not that much considering gas, food, and hotel rooms. Besides, we disagree. We think you deserve that and a whole lot more."

I just smiled and accepted it. I felt good about Jim, also. Even though I wasn't looking forward to driving all the way back by myself, I somehow seemed relieved that Jim had plans other than going back to the same life he had been living.

They all walked me out to the car as I took my bag and put it into the back seat. They shook my hand and told me their goodbyes with an invitation to come visit anytime I wanted.

Helen held out the uniform and said, "You should keep this so you will always remember this day."

I took the uniform knowing well that I would need no memento to remind me of this day. She hugged me and walked back inside behind Tiger and Cowboy, leaving Jim and I to say goodbye.

"I'll never be able to repay you for what you've done," he said,

"It was worth it," I replied, trying to keep the good-bye short as to prevent getting too emotional. "Good luck to you."

"You, too." I think Jim was thinking the same thing.

❧12❧

Driving away left me with mixed emotions. I was happy to be a part of this adventure and enjoyed meeting the people involved in Jim's story, but I felt lonely driving away by myself. It wasn't so much for the trip home but knowing that Jim had become a friend and a part of my life and I was saddened at the thought of not having him around.

I glanced down at the map setting on the seat beside me. I knew the way home without the map but I found myself looking at something different than the way home. Oakview, Wyoming was a little north and west of here so I made an odd decision. I concluded that it wouldn't be that much longer to go home that way.

I'm not sure why I wanted to drive back though there other than to say that perhaps I wasn't ready for this story to be over. It had lasted for so many years and I had only been involved in the very end so maybe I just wanted to extend it a little further.

Two hours later and I was driving past the school again.

The bleachers were still there with bits of paper scattered throughout the grass. The only people present now were a couple of guys who seemed to be cleaning up the grounds.

I slowly drove around and took in the sights of this little town.

I spotted a little diner and decided to stop and get me a soda before heading on. I walked in and sat at the bar. It was a common small town diner with ten stools along the bar that rested on swivel bases attached to the floor. There were only six tables which had four chairs each that adorned one wall with windows that ran the length of the diner.

"What'll you have?" An older woman was handing me a menu.

I think she was the only one working there and I was definitely the only customer.

"Just a coke, please," I replied.

She took a glass from beneath the bar and filled it up from a fountain dispenser behind her and handed it to me.

"Not from around here, are you?"

"No Ma'am," I said. "Alabama."

Before she could say anything, the door to the diner opened. I turned and looked and almost fell off the stool. It was Mandy, and not only had she seen me but was walking directly towards me.

"I thought that was you I saw in here."

"It's me," was my lame retort.

I felt like an ass running into her but as I looked into her eyes, I began to wonder if I hadn't secretly hoped to do that.

"Why are you still here?" she asked.

Good question. I didn't know what to day so I did what I had done since meeting her: I lied. "Oh, I had some other business up the road a piece but now I'm though for the day and heading back to Al...."

Whoops. That almost slipped out.

"Al?" she smiled. "Is that your boyfriend?"

"Ha ha," I faked. "No, I was going to say that I was heading back to Alpha Unit but I keep forgetting to drop the

Army lingo when I'm talking to civilians. I was heading back to base."

Tiger had coached me on what base to say I was from in case someone asked so I was prepared for that being her next question.

"Well, I'm glad I got to see you again. I wanted to apologize for earlier but you really caught me off guard."

"I'm sure."

"So, how long have you been in the Army?"

"I only have a few more weeks. I went in for two years right after high school on the G.I. Bill to help pay for college. I've already been taking some classes but now I can start full time."

That was sort of true in that I had checked out the G.I. Bill and considered it. Okay, it didn't make it true and I felt like a dog.

My sisters always joked about how honest a person I was and yet I couldn't carry on a conversation with this girl without telling one lie after another. It was making me sick to my stomach.

"So, then, you're not that much older than me."

The smile on her face when she said that gave me goose bumps. I couldn't remember the last time I had met someone to whom I was so immediately attracted. She was beautiful, intelligent, and funny.

I couldn't help but wonder what Jim, Tiger and Cowboy would think if they knew what was going on.

Sensing my concerns, she asked, "Do you want me to leave you alone?"

"No, no, no," I quickly rushed out.

"Okay," she smiled again. "If it had only been two 'nos' I might have wondered but three puts my mind to ease."

She was so easy to talk to. We sat there for 45 minutes

talking about everything and nothing. She finally told me that her parents were taking her to out to celebrate later that evening and she needed to go. I asked her for her number and address before she left and she gave them to me

"I expect to hear from you," she said as she walked toward the door of the diner.

"I promise you will."

I finished my coke and walked out to my car and started the long drive home. My mind was racing with all the memories of the day. I couldn't wait to contact Mandy. I wasn't sure if I would be able to tell Jim if and when I ever spoke with him again.

About halfway home I decided to stop and get a room for the night. I called home to give my mom an update and told her I would be home around 2:00 the next afternoon. I figured it would be closer to noon but I left myself some buffer room for Mom's sake.

When I got back home and started unpacking, I found an envelope in my bag with the Purple Heart inside and a note that read, "To remember me by."

I smiled as I thought about that crazy old guy.

I went back to work at the carwash and told everyone about the trip. Everything went back to normal except for no daily visits from Jim getting his seventy-five cents worth of gas.

I waited a month before calling Mandy so it would give me time to be out of my fictional tour of duty and be back home. I couldn't stand the thought of lying to her anymore. We talked for about 30 minutes and it was good to hear her voice. I told her that I was starting Auburn University in the fall which was completely true. She told me that she was going to the University of Wyoming in the fall where she planned to get a degree in Health Science and then she would try to go into medical school to become a doctor.

I had no doubt that she would be successful.

The months passed and we traded many letters over the summer, mainly because it was cheaper than calling long distance all the time. We continued to write after we started attending our respective colleges

I also received a letter about four months into school that Mom had forwarded to me. It had no return address but was postmarked from Idaho.

I was excited as I opened it knowing it had to be from Jim. It was. He told me that everyone was well and hoped that I was doing well, also. It didn't really say anything but it was good to read. It was signed by all three of them and by Tiger's wife, Helen, as well.

I always wondered if he realized that he had no return address on the envelope. Even though I had been to Tiger's home, I couldn't remember the street address to mail him back and I had tried to look it up but it must have been unlisted because I could never find it.

Mandy and I were going to see each other again right after the school year ended. We had planned it all year. Auburn got out for the summer three weeks before the University of Wyoming so I planned to drive up and see her while she was still in school. She wanted me to meet some of her new college friends and I knew I would be working all summer once I got home so it seemed like a perfect time.

As I drove up, I began to get excited the closer I got. Although we never got too intimate with our letters, there was always something there between the lines; little innuendos that at least gave me the hope that something more was there.

It was about 6 p.m. when I got to the campus. I followed the directions she had mailed to me and drove to her dorm.

It was an all girl's dorm so I had to wait in the lobby as they called up to her room.

The hall door opened and Mandy came running out and gave me a hug. Two other girls trailed behind her and she introduced them as her roommates.

"How was your trip?" she asked as she stepped back and let me breathe again.

"Piece of cake," I replied.

"You hungry?" she asked.

I said I was so the four of us walked to a restaurant down the block from her dorm.

"It's so good to see you," I said as we all sat down at a table.

"You, too," she replied.

"Are you glad to be out of the army?" one of her friends asked.

Oh no. Here we go again. It was obvious that she had told them how we met.

I just nodded and I think they could tell that I didn't want to discuss that because no one asked me anything else about it.

We ate dinner and talked about whatever came into our heads. They all laughed at my southern accent. It was a fun evening.

As it got later in the evening, Mandy's friends went back to the dorm and she rode with me to show me where I could get a hotel room for the night.

After checking in, I drove around to the room and carried my one small bag inside with me. I was only staying for one night so I hadn't packed a lot.

There was a small table with two chairs in the room and Mandy and I sat and talked by ourselves. It was fun meeting her friends but this was much nicer. There was certainly a bond between us and I knew that she felt it, too.

I couldn't help but wonder if she was the one. I do believe at that very moment I was in love with her.

As the night crept into early morning, she commented several times about it getting late and each time saying she probably should go. Each time I would ask if she wanted me to drive her back but each time she would add that she could stay a little longer. I didn't want the night to end and I think she felt the same way.

It ended with her falling asleep on the bed and I slept in one of the chairs.

I awoke the next morning with a stiff neck. It was already 10 o'clock and I was leaving around noon because I was starting work the next day at a company called Game Time that hired a lot of college kids for the summer.

I shook her gently and she woke up right away.

"What time is it?" she asked

"Ten o'clock."

"Why didn't you wake me earlier?"

"I just got up myself," I said.

She sat up and put on her shoes, which was the only thing she had taken off for the night.

I sat there watching her knowing that I had strong feelings for her. I knew also that our relationship had started on a lie and that it could never successfully continue as long as that existed between us.

"Mandy," I said, looking her intensely in the eyes. "There's something I have to tell you."

"What is it?" she asked with a puzzled look.

I motioned for her to sit down at the table as I did likewise. I wasn't sure if I was doing the right thing but I knew I couldn't stand lying to her anymore. I was equally divided on whether or not I should tell her but I convinced myself that Jim, Tiger and Cowboy deserved the credit for what they had done, so that was the deciding factor.

I began by telling her about my job at the car wash.

"I thought you were in the army," she said as she still looked confused.

"Please let me tell the whole story and then you can comment."

She smiled and nodded.

I told her everything, starting with Jim trying to get water to the story Jim had told me about her father. I could see her eyes tearing up as I talked about her dad. I continued and told her about the plan the three of them had devised after her father's death and about how I got involved including the fake Army uniform.

I told her everything.

When I finished, she sat with her head down and cried for several minutes.

I didn't know what to do.

"Going back into town was not part of the plan," I added. "I didn't expect to see you again. They never wanted you to know about any of this. I just never expected to like you so much and I couldn't bear to lie to you anymore."

She looked up and nodded. I went into the bathroom and grabbed the tissues from the sink and brought them to her. By the time she had regained her composure enough to talk again, it was already past noon.

"I don't know what to say to all this," she finally said.

"I know."

"I'm glad you told me, though.

"I was real young when he died but I still remember him. Mom had told me about the day they told her he'd been killed but she didn't tell me until I was old enough to understand. She said she attended a ceremony where they gave her a medal and told her it was for bravery under fire. She knew he had saved a life but we never knew the whole story until now.

"I guess you need to get going, huh?" she added.

I nodded and started packing my bag. We walked out to the car in silence and it continued all the way to her dorm.

I pulled up to the curb at the front of her dorm and walked around as she got out of the car.

"Thank you for telling me," she said again as she hugged me.

"You're welcome," I replied.

Then she turned and walked into the building and I got in the car and drove away.

It was a long drive home with nothing to think about except one thing: "Did I do the right thing?"

I kept playing it over and over in my mind. Part of me was upset that I could spoil such a wonderful night and part of me was glad to have it out in the open. But her reaction was so calm and her goodbye was so short. I wasn't sure what to make of it but it's all I could think about all the way home. It was torture.

I called her when I got home and we talked for a little while but I could tell it wasn't the same. We still wrote each other but the letters began to get further and further apart until one day they stopped altogether.

I finished the last two years of school without any contact with her.

I'm not sure what time I finally fell asleep but I awoke wearing the same clothes. The Nike box was sitting on the floor beside the bed and the Purple Heart was setting on the night stand.

I began to wonder how much of the story I had remembered before going to sleep and how much of it I had completed in my dreams.

I inhaled the smell of breakfast coming down the hallway into my bedroom. My dad was famous for his Saturday morning meal.

I walked into the kitchen as he was putting the finishing touches on this savory masterpiece which consisted of western style omelets, grits, homemade biscuits, gravy, bacon and sausage, fresh sliced tomatoes and the best hash browns you'll ever eat.

I pulled up a seat as Mom poured me a glass of orange juice.

I sat there and ate in silence as I thought more about those events from the past and wondered how Jim and Mandy were doing. I had thought about Mandy many times and had fought the urge to try and contact her over the years. I could only assume she graduated from Medical school and was a practicing doctor. I imagined her with a husband and kids and could only hope she was happy.

I was more upset with Jim. How could he not stay in touch? As I thought about it, however, it made sense with him. He was a closed book. I was lucky enough to read a few pages but in the end, he needed to be alone. It made me sad for him.

Later in the day, Dad asked me to help him put a new roof on the pump house, which I did. Then he and I played cards and argued.

Then I went to see Granny.

"My God, how much do you weigh now?"

It was a typical greeting.

"About the same as always," I said, defending myself as usual.

Granny offered to cook me lunch if I would take her fishing so I agreed. I'm still not sure what it was she cooked but it was definitely some type of meat.

Dad had dug out a small pond several years earlier down below the new house and had stocked it with catfish and bass which he had caught from other ponds. This was convenient because Granny didn't care where she fished as long as she caught something that provided her with a free meal.

I got her fishing rod and helped her into my car to take her to the pond. I stopped back at Mom's house and picked up a cooler so we could take some drinks and have something to serve as a chair. We took some chicken liver which is Granny's favorite bait to use and catfish love it.

I set the cooler by the water, took off my shirt to keep cool and sat on the cooler. Granny sat beside me. I took a piece of chicken liver and cut it into small pieces so it would stay on the hook better and cast out my line.

Granny always liked to use the entire piece of liver because she thought it would attract a bigger fish. Either that or she figured if she couldn't catch a fish, maybe she could knock it unconscious.

I was watching my line as she went to cast hers out into the water. I could tell from the sound, however, that her timing was off and the bait went straight up into the air. I tensed up knowing that it would have to come back down, which it did, striking me square on the top of my shoulder. Then this incredibly large, slimy chunk of liver proceeded to slide down my back and finally came to rest on Granny's leg.

Granny looked all around for it and finally saw it on her leg. "Look where that landed." she laughed.

"I know darn well where it landed," I said turning my back to her so she could see the long slimy trail. "Now wipe me off."

She laughed so hard she nearly fell off the cooler.

We caught several catfish and I took them back to her house and cleaned them for her so she could cook them later in the week.

The rest of my weekend was a typical visit. I got together with some old friends from high school and saw everyone in the family.

I left to go back home around five o'clock Sunday afternoon, telling my parents goodbye and promising Mom I would call when I got home. As I drove off the mountain toward Fort Payne, I decided to stop by the car wash to get gas before getting on the interstate.

I pulled up to the self-service pumps and filled up. Upon paying for the gas, the young attendant asked if I would like a car wash.

"Sure," I replied, realizing that I had never paid for a wash before.

I pulled up onto the tracks as another young attendant guided me forward. He handed me a damp cloth explaining it was for my dash and asked me to keep the automobile in neutral. I do believe he was reading from the exact same script used when I worked here. He flipped the switch and a roller popped up and pushed me through the wash.

This was the first time I had gone through the wash area since I had worked here. Everything looked so familiar. It was as if it had only been a few weeks ago. There was the Midder curtain in all its splendor with its twenty-seven grease fittings and then came the giant blow dryer at the end.

Leaving the wash building, I turned onto Main Street and headed out of town.

Suddenly I had an urge to make one more stop. As I retraced the same turns I had taken so many years ago, I began to question the sanity of this decision, but still I drove onward.

As I pulled into the driveway of the house of Jim's sister, I noticed that the old wood siding had been replaced with bright green vinyl siding. Other than that, the place looked pretty much the same as I remembered. The hanging plants still adorned the eve of the porch ceiling, only this time they were in full bloom.

I knew that it was possible that she didn't live here anymore.

I strolled up the steps to the porch and knocked on the door. The door opened and there stood the redneck. He hadn't changed much. Only a little spot of gray on each side of his beard offered any hint of change at all. I could swear he was wearing the same flannel shirt, jeans, and work boots that he had on fifteen years ago.

"Can I help you?" he asked.

"Is Thelma here?"

"She ran down to the store to get some milk. She should be back in a minute," he answered. He was looking at me with a squint in his eyes. "Hey! Don't I know you?"

"I came by here several years ago with Jim," I said, figuring it would be best to let him know right from the start.

"That's right. Leo, isn't it? How the heck have you been? Come in. Come in. Want a beer?"

I was absolutely stunned.

He got me a beer from the fridge and asked me to sit at the table. Good thing, too, because his kindness had me shaken up. He sat there with me and talked my head off as if we had been best friends for a long time.

A few moments later, Thelma came in carrying a gallon jug of milk.

"Look who's here," the redneck proclaimed. "It's Leo, Jim's old friend."

"Leo. Hello. How have you been?"

She placed the milk in the fridge and sat down there with us. Her hair was completely gray now. She didn't look old as much as she looked tired. She still displayed the same genuine goodness I had seen in her before.

"How's Jim?" I asked.

"Jim is doing great. Him and some friends went into business together and apparently are doing rather well."

"Apparently nothing," the redneck interrupted. "He's rich."

"I don't know about being rich," Thelma continued, "but he seems to be doing very well. He came down Christmas before last and brought his girlfriend. He has bought a house and I think she is living with him."

I couldn't believe what I was hearing but I was sure glad to be hearing it

"Girlfriend?" I asked. "Tell me about her."

"I don't know what to say, really. She seemed really nice, didn't you think?" she looked at her redneck husband.

"She was a sweetie. They made such an adorable couple." He was still smiling from ear to ear.

"Okay," I said. "Who is this man and what have you done with your husband?"

Thelma smiled but the redneck almost sprayed beer he laughed so hard.

"Jim had been telling us about her for months before they came to visit," Thelma continued. "I think she worked for him at one time. She's about his age and I believe she said her family came here from Guatemala."

"Worked for him? What kind of business did they go into?" I asked.

"They own a whole chain of clothing stores," the redneck answered.

Thinking he might be exaggerating, I looked to Thelma for confirmation. She was nodding her head. "They own several Army surplus stores. It started with one store in Idaho Falls but now they own eight stores in several states."

I smiled as I thought of Big Al's Army Surplus store. I wondered if that was the first one they had owned.

"Wait a minute," Thelma suddenly said. "Are you sure you don't know about this?"

"No. I haven't heard from Jim since I was in college and that's been ten years ago. Why do you say that?" I asked.

"Because Jim sent me a newspaper clipping about six months ago. Hold on. I'll be right back."

She got up and went into her bedroom and came back with a photo album. She had a strange smile on her face as she flipped through the pages until she came to the page she was looking for and handed me the book.

The newspaper clipping took up almost the entire page

behind the protective plastic cover,

I could tell right away that the picture was Jim, Tiger and Cowboy standing in front of a store with a banner on the front window which read, "Grand Opening."

The caption beneath the picture read, "Three veterans are still making a living from Uncle Sam. Pictured above are Jim TerreII, Willie Richards and Mitchell Bengal as they commemorate the grand opening of their eighth Army surplus store. They operate seven other successful locations across the Northwest."

"That's great," I said.

Thelma was still looking at me as if waiting for a different response.

I begin to think that I was missing something so I looked at the picture again and then I saw it. The sign on top of the building read, "LEO'S ARMY SURPLUS #8."

www.ingramcontent.com/pod-product-compliance
Lightning Source LLC
Chambersburg PA
CBHW030631130626
46552CB00002B/790